D0597509

THE QUICK
AND THE DEAD

THE QUICK
AND THE DEAD

Judy Gardiner

St. Martin's Press
New York

Copyright © 1981 by Judy Gardiner
For information, write: St. Martin's Press,
175 Fifth Avenue, New York, N.Y. 10010
Manufactured in the United States of America

Library of Congress Cataloging in Publication Data

Gardiner, Judy, 1922-
The quick and the dead.

I. Title.
PR6057.A627Q5   1982   823'.914   81-18213
ISBN 0-312-66050-2   AACR2

To Shirley Russell

THE QUICK
AND THE DEAD

I
THE FACE

1

The Reverend Arthur Parsloe was a large, looming man with restless eyes and a lot of crooked teeth that gave him a cluttered look. Patting cake crumbs from the front of his grey cardigan he hauled himself up in his chair and demanded to know what had induced a nice young woman like Eleanor Millard to hide herself away in a place like Jackdaw's Cottage.

'Now, Arthur,' remonstrated his wife from behind the tea tray, 'I'm perfectly sure that Mrs Millard knows what she's doing, so pass me your cup and saucer if you want some more tea.'

'Stuck at the end of a soggy lane in a pile of old rotting timbers – no more tea, thank you – can be good for neither mind nor body. Loneliness corrodes the brain even as damp induces respiratory disorders and a tendency to fungoid growth on the soles of the feet.'

Sitting opposite him, Eleanor Millard smiled. It was an attractive smile, with no more than a hint of steel.

'I live there because I like it,' she said. 'And I don't think you can have seen the place recently, Mr Parsloe. The people I bought it from had it restored very carefully, and although it's got all the normal labour-saving gadgets they don't interfere with its character. It's still got its charming old crooked walls, and—'

'And tell me, dear Mrs Ah, what can possibly be charming about a crooked wall?' the vicar demanded pettishly. 'Walls should be straight, in order that they may be used for hanging pictures on, or for building bookshelves against, or, in moments of stress, for propping up the human frame. The love of crooked walls and tilting floors is pure affecta-

9

tion, on a par with professed fondness for liquefying Camembert and abstract art.'

'My floors don't tilt,' Eleanor said mildly, and the vicar flung her a challenging look.

'My floors – my roof – my house – dear Lord, will we never break free from the ignominious lust for possession? Why can't we all live in sensible and utilitarian little units like bees? Some sort of neat ferro-concrete honeycomb should be quite sufficient for anyone, provided it's warm and dry and equipped with a few useful amenities.'

'My husband and I spent ten years in a concrete honeycomb,' Eleanor said. 'We lived in a flat that the average worker bee would probably have felt quite at home in, and the school where we both taught was another featureless slab overlooking a lot of grass and no trees. It didn't convince either of us that uniformity is necessarily a good thing.'

'There you are, Arthur,' cried Mrs Parsloe, a small brown bun of a woman. 'You will get on your hobby-horse, won't you? Serves you right when someone comes along and knocks you off.'

'I hope I didn't sound aggressive—'

'Quite right, quite right,' the vicar said, suddenly cheerful, 'nothing worse than an aggressive woman, unless it's a sloppy one mooning and mimping over the dust of ages. You should see the rubbish that gets sold at the church bazaar each year.'

'My husband is rather opposed to antiquity,' confided Mrs Parsloe as if he wasn't there. 'I think it's something to do with years of living in old and uncomfortable vicarages. Never once have we had the benefit of main drainage, and in this one we've never succeeded in tracing the septic tank at all. For all I know we haven't even got one. The Diocesan Board does what it can, of course, but when the wind settles in the north-east life is rather trying.'

Eleanor nodded sympathetically, and glanced round the ramshackle room with its worn furniture and dusty books before replacing her cup and saucer on the tea tray with murmured thanks. She stood up.

'So in what way can I be of assistance to you?' asked the

Reverend Parsloe.

'As I mentioned in my letter, I'd be very grateful if you could help me trace the history of Jackdaw's Cottage. I thought perhaps the parish records might have something.'

'Possibly. What about the deeds?'

'They only go back to 1800 and the cottage is four centuries old. You see,' she said earnestly, 'I want to find out about the people who lived there. It's probably asking a lot but I want to know their names, and I want to know how they lived and what happened to them. And I also want to know how they fitted in with the history that was going on outside. How did they feel when Elizabeth Tudor died, for instance, and what did the later ones think of the Protectorate, or of Napoleon? Did any of them fight in the Crimean War? If only I could gather sufficient material I'd like to write a book about them all – only for my own amusement, of course—' She halted, as if she had betrayed herself too much and too soon.

'Does Mr Millard share your enthusiasm for history?' enquired the vicar's wife.

Eleanor Millard stiffened slightly, like someone feeling a twinge of pain. 'My husband died two years ago.'

No one spoke. Only Mrs Parsloe bowed her head for a moment in what could have been a token expression of sympathy while Eleanor stared hard at a hole in the carpet and wondered what had made it. A large mouse perhaps, or even a small rat . . .

'He was thirty-four,' she said finally, when it became obvious that they were expecting her to say something more. 'It took a long while to face up to it, and afterwards I went on trying to live the same way as before. I stayed on at the flat and went on teaching at the same school, but it didn't really work. Keeping busy helped over the initial stage, but teaching's a hard job and whenever I was tired I found myself sinking into a self-pity that I couldn't shake off. It occurred to me then that I needed to get away to sort things out – to sort myself out, I suppose I mean – so I gave in my notice and a week later saw the advertisement for the cottage in a Sunday paper and bought it.'

Impulsively the vicar's wife got out of her chair and went

11

across to her. For a moment she looked as if she wanted to enfold the younger woman in the way that one enfolds a hurt child. Instead, she touched her arm with an awkward little movement and said: 'Oh, my dear . . . '

'And is solitude having the hoped-for effect?' asked the vicar, also rising to his feet.

'I sleep better, so I think it must be.'

'Ah well,' he said with sudden animation, 'off to the vestry to see what we can find . . . '

Saying goodbye to Mrs Parsloe, Eleanor followed him out of the vicarage and into the big tangled garden. Wood pigeons were purring in the trees and butterflies hovered among the self-sown flowers. They walked down a rough-mown path towards a gate in the churchyard wall without speaking. Increasingly she had the impression that he found her trivial and a bore.

In comparison to the rambling Victorian house the Norman church was very small and very bare. It smelt of damp stone and dusty hassocks, and the bunch of flowers standing in a jug by the chancel steps had already dropped most of its petals. In the vicinity of the font the vicar halted so abruptly that she almost collided with him.

'And what about the atmosphere in here?' he demanded hoarsely. 'As someone with a sense of history and a sentimental attachment to old buildings, what d'you make of this place, Mrs Ah?'

Startled, she could only murmur that it seemed very peaceful. The vicar snorted and led the way to the vestry.

'I have to admit that I'm not a regular communicant,' she said, following him. 'I've tried, but—'

'More than you can say for most of my parishioners. They don't even bother with weddings, christenings and funerals any more. Oh, they're busy enough in the parish hall with their coffee mornings and jumble sales, but if you find my church peaceful, Mrs Er—' He stopped again, looming over her like a large grey cloud, 'it's the peace of death. No one ever comes unless it's to do a brass rubbing or to find out who used to live in their old house. If they feel like rejoicing they go to the pub and if they're in trouble they see either their doctor or their bank manager. They rarely come to me.'

'Perhaps they're afraid of you,' she suggested gently.

He shook his head. 'Merely indifferent.'

The vestry was small and dark and he switched on the unshaded light that hung lonely as a dewdrop over the table. Unlocking the deal cupboard that stood against the wall he rummaged within it for a moment or two, then to Eleanor's surprise produced a bottle and a glass tumbler.

'I drink,' he said.

'Oh.' She could think of nothing useful to add.

'Sorry there's only one glass,' he said, splashing whisky into it. 'You take that side, I'll take this.'

She began to decline his offer then changed her mind, unwilling to appear prim.

'Salutations,' he said, and after her one polite sip twitched the glass from her fingers and drained it.

Restored, he turned back to the cupboard and hunted through a pile of old leather-bound books, two of which he dragged out and banged down in front of her. Dust rose in the still air.

'1715 to 1739 . . . 1676 to 1691 – might have something. What's the name of the chap you're interested in?'

'I don't know his name,' Eleanor said patiently. 'I'm trying to discover it.'

'Went to fight in the Crimea, did you say?'

'No. The man who built Jackdaw's Cottage. I want to start with him.'

It was as if she had never written her preliminary letter, carefully setting out the questions that interested her most. It seemed then as if they had never even had the rather stilted little tea-time conversation with Mrs Parsloe presiding behind the teapot and the Victoria sandwich.

'How old's the house?'

'I can't say with any exactitude. I only know that it's somewhere in the region of four hundred years.'

'1580,' the vicar said, browsing. 'Before the death of Elizabeth and long before the burning of the last heretics in England.' He began to read aloud: ' "In the year of our Lord 1641 was drowned in Templeton Brook one Hannah Maria Fiskin, spinster of this Parish, who pleaded guilty to

13

divers charges of witchcraft, namely, to making an effigy of one Matthew William Jessop with a view to bringing about his untimely demise . . . " '

'They drowned her deliberately?' Eleanor stared over his shoulder at the pale spider-leg writing. 'I've heard about such things, but to meet them here, in cold blood—'

'Hideous reading indeed,' he said, turning the pages. ' "Thomas Fowler, an honest old man of this Parish, buried on April 10 1784" – that's no use to you, is it? – "Eliza Crumpe, pauper, buried on the north side of the church . . . " ' He paused and looked at her sharply. 'You understand what that means?'

She returned his gaze. In the melancholy light their faces suddenly had a strained, ashen quality.

'No,' she said quietly. 'I'm afraid I don't.'

'The north side of the church was supposed to belong to the devil, so presumably paupers were regarded as part of his collection. As men die, so shall they arise; if in the faith of the Lord, towards the south, and shall arise in Glory; if in unbelief, towards the north, then they are past all hope...' The Reverend Parsloe slopped some more whisky into the tumbler and drank it briskly. 'Ah well, savage but unequivocal. People knew where they stood in those days.'

'Thanks to the power of the clergy,' Eleanor said, then added a little less sharply: 'But if you can't find anything that relates to my cottage – I mean, if this is taking up too much of your time, Mr Parsloe, perhaps you could let me search through the parish registers on my own?'

With an abrupt gesture he snapped the book shut. 'It would take months to go through all these entries and on the advice of my archdeacon I'm afraid that it isn't possible to allow the laity unrestricted access to valuable church property. In any case,' he turned back to the cupboard, 'our records don't go back beyond 1640. You can see for yourself.'

You could have told me that in the first place, she thought, and heard herself thanking him and apologising for any trouble she had caused.

'No trouble,' he said. 'But if you're determined to pursue your romantic quest I suggest that you contact the County

14

Record Office. I believe they go in for hoarding all the old rubbish that should by rights have been burned the moment it ceased to have any practical value.'

When he had cleared the table of books, whisky bottle and tumbler he relocked the cupboard and pocketed the key. Leaning against the opposite wall she said thoughtfully: 'Is the lack of a congregation the only reason for your despair?'

'I drink because I happen to like the taste,' he said, and led the way out of the vestry to where sunlight was dancing through the open door.

'Thank you for your help, Mr Parsloe,' Eleanor said, and opened the clasp of her handbag. 'Is there a fee to pay?'

'Normally yes, but we'll overlook it this time.' He smiled at her with sudden and unexpected sweetness, waited until she had closed her handbag again, and then added: 'But of course, a little something in the offertory box would be more than welcome.'

Her two fifty pence pieces fell into it with a hollow thud.

They walked slowly through the graveyard, and obeying a sudden impulse she bent down and ran her hand over the tussocky grass that covered an unobtrusive mound in the earth.

'He might be buried here, for all we know.'

'Who might?' It was obvious by now that he was being deliberately obtuse.

'The man who built my cottage.' Instinctively she looked up to see where the shadow of the church fell.

'This is the south side,' he said dryly. 'The side the spirits made just.'

'And of course, this will be the right side for him.'

'How do you know?'

She walked over to the lychgate, opened it and then turned to look at him. 'Because the cottage is so beautiful. Goodbye, Mr Parsloe.'

Without speaking he turned and walked away through the rustling grass, threading his way between leaning headstones and lichened sepulchres, then abruptly he turned and began to hurry back towards the road, stumbling and clumsily waving his arms.

15

But she had already driven away and he stood motionless, staring dolefully into space while he fumbled in his pocket for a peppermint before returning to the vicarage.

2

She drove home, turning down the narrow lane and negotiating the potholes with care. Fields stretched away on either side, and nearer the farm a small herd of pigs rootled and squealed in a wired enclosure. Rounding a bend she met the farmer's wife, a fat pink woman flapping along in plimsolls and carrying a bucket of mash. She grinned when she saw Eleanor, and set down the bucket in preparation for a chat.

'Nice weather keeps on, Mrs Millard!'

Eleanor slowed to a standstill and agreed that it did. The woman leaned comfortably against the side of the car and contemplated Eleanor at leisure. Her brass-coloured hair was caught back in an elastic band and she smelt of sweat.

'Not fed up with country ways yet?'

'Certainly not,' Eleanor said, smiling. 'It gets better every day.'

'Nice in the summer but you might get a bit fed up in the winter. That's why the other people sold up – couldn't stand the long winter months.'

'I don't think they'll bother me, Mrs Lacey.'

'Maybe you'll get a friend or two to stay with you.'

'Maybe,' Eleanor agreed.

'Of course, the country's nothing like it was,' went on Mrs Lacey. 'Everyone's on the electric now, and all the old cottages no one'd live in if you paid 'em are all primped up like little palaces. Makes you laugh, really. I mean, I hear that the folk who bought Sworder's ole place have got a swimming pool with proper warm water in it down where the ole blackcurrant bushes used to be, and they go swimming without their costumes on and get up to all manner of high jinks and don't care if other people catch 'em at it, neither...' Her voice droned on, homely as a singing kettle. 'Funny, when you come to think of it. Like there's us ole locals still blessing the day we got mains water laid on, and then there's the city people that bought Barrow Farm going to dear knows what expense to have a well bored in their garden because they reckon what comes out the mains ain't pure. Bin used five times before, they reckon. So they got a water diviner all the way from Wales, I'm told, and that cost them a packet because he stayed best part of a week, running all about with his little hazel twig, but they're as happy as larks now they have to cart all their water in buckets just like Mum and Dad used to. Doris Pitts says they only ever eat brown bread.'

'Times change,' Eleanor said.

'Times change, but folks don't,' observed Mrs Lacey, thoughtfully scratching her shoulder. 'They're never satisfied for long, but what it all boils down to is this; it's what you are, not what you got.'

'I quite agree,' Eleanor said. 'But sometimes I'd give a lot to know whether it's true to say that people have always been the same.'

'Course they have.' Mrs Lacey stopped scratching and fixed Eleanor with bright blue eyes. 'They might wear different clothes and eat different things, but underneath they've always bin the same.'

'In 1641 they drowned a woman in Templeton Brook because they thought she was a witch,' replied Eleanor, thinking back to the Reverend Parsloe.

'And they're still killing people for being Catholics or Protestants or Communists or whatever,' the farmer's wife said. 'Whatever age it is, they don't seem to come no better.'

'You don't appear to have much time for the human race, Mrs Lacey.'

'Oh, I like the ones I know. It's the ones you see on the news I can't abide. . .'

They laughed, and Eleanor restarted the car while over in the field the pigs got wind of the mash and began to shriek.

Two months' sojourn at the cottage had made her familiar with every twist and turn of the lane. Lonely and remote, it had been given a hard surface during the war when the Americans had opened a small bomber station nearby, but the concrete had long ago become cracked and split by the power of the weather and the insidious thrusting of tree roots. In places, the branches met overhead, and now their pattern lay on the ground in a quivering mesh of black and gold. An old weatherboard barn, collapsed beyond redemption, marked the southern boundary of the Lacey farmland and was the only other building within a mile, such wartime ephemera as Nissen huts having disappeared without trace many years ago.

She drove slowly, resting her arm on the open window and savouring the delight of returning home. It never failed her, this sense of home-coming, even if she had only been to the farm to collect the mail and her daily pint of milk.

After the final bend the lane began its gradual descent to the small valley where Jackdaw's Cottage lay against its background of high blue-green corn as if it too had grown from a seed.

She stopped the car and sat looking at it for a moment, her loving eyes noting each curve of the massive timbers, each ripple of the peg-tiled roof and the way in which the small-paned windows seemed to look back at her with a sleepy, heavy-lidded smile of welcome. She had never owned a house before, and to own one as beautiful and as historic as this seemed to fill her with constant amazement. She thought, a trifle wryly, that her reaction could probably only be matched by that of a woman who had recently borne a first child.

Leaving the car she walked through the small front gate and along the paved path flanked on either side by clipped mounds of aromatic box. The garden with its tangle of lavender and old roses lay motionless in the July heat and the cottage itself felt cool by comparison. She wandered through it, opening windows in the big sitting-room with its open fireplace banked with flowers and its polished elm staircase, and the little dining-room she had furnished with an old refectory table and stickback chairs she had bought at an auction.

It was beautiful. Beautiful and calm and faintly mysterious. Mingled with the scent of roses was the not unpleasant under-smell of wood preservative and new carpeting. She was proud of the new carpet, a plain pale lemon in colour and made of nylon, which wouldn't attract moth.

She sat down, stroking her skirt over her knees and feeling conscious that she, a passable-looking widow in her mid-thirties, blended very satisfactorily with her background. She thought that she might make a pot of tea, then realised that it was too late for tea and too early for sherry. It was an empty hour; a time for sitting still and allowing the ghosts of centuries to take quiet and comfortable possession.

Which led her back to the somewhat abortive interview with the Reverend Parsloe, and to his suggestion that the County Record Office might be able to throw some historical light on the cottage.

She went across to the phone, wedging herself on the edge of the table while she consulted the directory and hoped that the office hadn't already closed for the day.

'Good afternoon, this is a Mrs Eleanor Millard,' she said, 'and I would like to trace something of the history of an old property that I recently purchased in Asham Parva. The name is Jackdaw's—'

The voice asked her to hold the line for a moment and Eleanor waited, smiling a little.

'Asham Parva?' said another voice, briskly businesslike, 'and the name is Mrs Millard? We will do our best to help you, Mrs Millard, if you would care to make an appointment to visit the students' room any weekday between the hours of 10 a.m. and 5.30 p.m.'

Expressing her thanks, Eleanor arranged to be there at 11.15 on the following morning. And then decided that it was time for a sherry after all.

Evening came slowly, bringing with it a wisp of breeze that stirred the treetops and twitched at the curtains like an invisible hand. With the refectory table prettily laid for one, she finished mixing the salad while her lamb chop grilled, then washed and dried a peach and placed it in the centre of a small blue and white Spode dish. She ate slowly and thoughtfully, relishing the quietness and watching the dying sun stain the white walls pink. My walls, she thought. My chimneys, my strong sheltering roof. . .The Reverend Parsloe had criticised her possessiveness, but was it in fact such a bad thing to love one's home?

During her early years, home-making had been taken care of by Mother in terms of cream enamel and cotton rep, and she had hardly noticed the transfer to brick, glass and cobblestones-in-cement when she went up to university. She had worked hard, and most Wednesday evenings played squash rackets with a fellow student called Mona Butterwood and cried with a kind of squeamish rage when a post-graduate from the Philosophy Department made an attempt on her virginity. Mona told her that all men were bastards, and for the rest of the term Eleanor was happy to believe her. They went on a walking tour of Scotland where it rained every day; both caught colds and had a sudden and extraordinarily violent row because Mona believed Eleanor to have swiped her Beecham's Powders. They parted at Inverary with aching feet and running noses, Eleanor heading for home while Mona declared her intention of sticking to the original itinerary and getting as far as Ullapool.

At the beginning of Eleanor's third year her mother died, and watching her father's quiet confusion as he struggled to make his own bed and to understand the intricacies of the vacuum cleaner and its attachments, she thought seriously of giving up her course and taking a daily job from home. But he refused her offer, when she made it, with unusual firmness, and shortly afterwards removed himself to a Septembertide Home on the Isle of Wight where he made a number of friends and developed an unsuspected talent for amateur theatricals and two-handed brag. He didn't need her, but sent her a postcard view of Ventnor to congratulate her on gaining an Honours Degree in Modern English. After that she was on her own, a tall, rather gangling girl with big feet and thoughtful eyes behind pale-rimmed glasses. She tried journalism and found it trivial beyond endurance, then took a job in the library of the

20

Imperial War Museum where the cramped conditions and endless preoccupation with slaughter gave her migraine. The idea of teaching came gradually; children both frightened and attracted her, and when the doctor who was treating her headaches suggested that she needed a change and a job with more variety she applied on the spur of the moment for a post at a new comprehensive in Outer London, and was very surprised when she learned that she had got it.

The noise, the crowds and the atmosphere of cheerful philistinism appalled her at first, and it was not until she had been driven to lose her temper and lash her class with a fluent vituperation which delighted them as much as it astonished her that she was able to feel in control of the situation. And with the realisation of her ascendency came a wonderful vivid pleasure in the career she had finally chosen.

She had been at the school for three weeks when she encountered Mo Millard at a staff meeting at which they had both volunteered to go on a day trip to Boulogne with a group of thirteen-year-olds. Dodging his offer to drive her home afterwards, she allowed him to drop her off at the bus stop where she stood thinking over their conversation about educational research and watching with a strange disappointment the tail lights of his MG wink away into the distance.

A week later he invited her out for a drink, and before the evening was over she had fallen madly in love for the first time in her life.

He was a large New Zealander with a curly close-fitting beard and happy blue eyes below an already receding hairline. As a biology teacher he had a casual, rather throwaway style and a huge booming laugh that could be heard three classrooms away, and although his pupils addressed him openly as Milly they paid him a high degree of attention. Drinking lager with him beneath the tumult of a jukebox she discovered that he was hoping to take a year's sabbatical in order to write a textbook on algae.

'The big bladder-wracks and kelps are really my scene,' he bawled in her ear. 'I've loved them since I was a kid, and

21

of course it'll mean a trip to the Sargasso Sea where there are hundreds of lovely square miles of them all waiting for some crazy coot like me . . . '

His shining enthusiasm made her laugh, then suddenly she found that it was very easy to become delighted by the thought of seaweed; in a high shriek she told him how she had collected it in a little tin bucket as a child on holiday, and how much she had enjoyed popping the bubbles in it.

He went to the bar to refill their tankards, and was halfway through asking her whether she realised that both Fucus and Laminaria possessed unicellular reproductive organs when the record on the jukebox came to an end and his voice exploded through the pub with all the power of a pneumatic drill.

No, she said, almost weeping with laughter, no, she hadn't realised it, and he seized her hand across the table and told her solemnly that the responsibility of this new knowledge could only make her a larger and finer woman. His hand was warm and dry, and her own lay within it like a quiveringly acquiescent little animal.

They left the pub and in the close confines of the MG his physical presence overwhelmed her. It was as if she were turning into another person.

He drove her home, and while she was still tormented by the problem of whether or not to invite him up to the flat she found him there beside her, with the pitiless glare of the centre light illuminating the toast crumbs that still sprinkled the table from breakfast. Hurriedly she switched it off, and when he put his arm round her shoulders and walked with her to the bed-settee she cried in vexation that that wasn't what she meant. She hadn't meant that at all.

'Of course not,' he agreed, and made love to her very gently and considerately. And perhaps because of having waited for so long, the tumultuous rush of feeling was almost more than she could stand. She bit his bare shoulder, and the salty taste drove her mad with another sort of love. A love for him, and not merely for what he was doing to her.

And afterwards – she had often read about the after-wards sensation of disappointment and absurdity, and despite her passionate happiness was partly prepared for a sudden bleak return to the common things. Someone had once written that a man's contempt for a woman can begin the moment he withdraws from her, and if it was going to be like that then she determined that she too would play it that way. She would look at him as if he were a total stranger, even maybe bring herself to hurl a shoe at his retreating back before the tears of pain poured from her eyes.

But it wasn't at all like that. He lay by her side, stroking her flat white belly and saying: 'It was the first time, wasn't it? The very first time. . .'

'Yes,' she said. 'How did you know?'

'Difficult to say,' he said, still stroking. 'Sort of – well, a bit like—'

'Popping seaweed,' she suggested, and under his hand her belly began to quiver with happy laughter.

And it was all happiness. They got up to make two mugs of instant coffee and Mo found a packet of biscuits in the cupboard. They took them back to bed, and when she woke in the morning he was having a bath and she rolled over on to his share of the pillow and thought I'm so in love I could die. . .

They lived together for three months before they married, and although neither of them had any family present at the ceremony – Eleanor's father was ill with bronchitis – the dinginess of the day and the register office was made bright by half a dozen vociferous friends from the school and Eleanor's class made her a huge floral structure of swans towing a gondola across a blue plastic tea tray.

Love did a lot for her. It made her poised yet more friendly, and her feet didn't seem so big. And when Mo suggested that she should dispense with her glasses and wear contact lenses instead, she made an appointment to consult the optician on the following day.

They moved to a larger flat merely because they needed more space. Neither of them had much in the way of furniture, and Eleanor went shopping one lunchtime for rugs and ready-made curtains, then as an afterthought purchased a few more knives and forks from Woolworths. Their chief concern was the big square table at which they

23

could mark homework, write reports and plan various school projects. Once Eleanor raised her head from a pile of exercise books and looked across at Mo: 'Hey, when are you going to the Sargasso Sea?'

He looked blank for a moment, then smiled. 'Operation temporarily suspended.'

'So long as it *is* only temporary.'

'Want to get rid of me?'

'No,' she said. 'It's just that I don't want you to give anything up because of me.'

'I'll do it one day,' he said. 'Lots of time for things like that.'

But of course there wasn't. Within twelve months he was complaining of tiredness and a pain in his back. The doctor found nothing wrong, but suggested that he should give up some of his out-of-school activities such as Nature Trails and all-night badger-watching. He refused, until he found that he could no longer carry on. The pains spread, increasing in severity, and a week's sojourn in hospital resulted in a diagnosis of cancer. They told Eleanor while Mo was dressing to go home and the doctor patted her shoulder and said sit down for a moment. No need to hurry. . .

She didn't believe it. Staring dry-mouthed at the opposite wall she said that men of her husband's age and constitution didn't develop things like cancer but even supposing there was just a suspicion of it, cancer could be cured these days, couldn't it? It was then they had to break the news that it was inoperable.

She walked back to the ward with her head held high and when Mo insisted on carrying his suitcase she let him, rather than give him the slightest suspicion that all was not as it should be. He died ten months later, propped in her arms with his poor brittle bones sharp against her breast while he kept whispering *'Never mind, love. . .never mind. . .'* as if he were trying to console her for something of no more than trivial importance.

For a while it seemed as if she had died with him. Although the Head offered her a full term's leave of absence with pay she continued to teach, accepting with a frozen smile the awkward condolences of the staff and the

24

little stumbled tributes paid by his pupils. She watched while notices handwritten by him became gradually out of date and were replaced by new ones, and she shook hands with the new biology teacher who had been engaged to fill his vacancy: a fat man called Fleming, who was only five years off retirement.

It was not until she began to break out of the ice that she started to take notice of things, rather than people. She saw the blue and white Spode dish which now held the remains of her suppertime peach in a junk-shop window, and on impulse went in and bought it. Its cool beauty appealed to her, and to search shop windows for another one to match it was one way of passsing the leaden weekends. Eventually she found three more, two of them slightly chipped, but she couldn't get over the difference they made to the room, spaced along the top shelf of the bookcase.

She became aware of colour. Of patterns and textures, and she realised that at this particularly crucial stage of her life it was wise to indulge herself a little. Her mother had left her a sum of several thousand pounds which was still intact in a deposit account, and she began to widen her interest to antiques of all kinds. Throwing away the old Woolworth cutlery which she and Mo had always found adequate she bought four place settings in heavy Edwardian silver. She bought a small Kasak rug in glowing jewel colours which made the two modern armchairs appear distinctly ill at ease, so she replaced them with a couple of Victorian button-backs which she had recovered, one at a time, in velvet.

And when she came home from school it was to sit marking exercise books at her most extravagant purchase so far: an eighteenth-century Pembroke table with a cross-banded top and brass castors. The beauty of her new possessions brought her comfort, and compensated in some small degree for a life without Mo.

But teaching was no longer the same. Now a well-groomed and rather fastidious woman in her early thirties she began to suspect that the light had gone out of her work as well as her private life. The noise of the children, their brash tastes and aggressive instincts, began to irritate her.

She felt alienated from them in the same way that she knew herself to be alienated from the rest of the staff as the teacher they couldn't go on feeling sorry for indefinitely. She didn't want them to feel sorry for her, yet knew as well as they did that it was impossible to behave as if the tragedy of Mo's dying had never happened. Sometimes it seemed as if the most tactful thing she could do would be to remove herself to another school. Yet she clung on, sick of the same faces and the same routine, yet unable to cut herself off from the place where Mo had worked, towering above the others and filling the corridors with his cheerful explosions of laughter.

The end came when the Head asked her if she would take charge of a coachload of O-level students on a trip to Stratford-on-Avon during the Easter holidays. She refused, saying that she had already made arrangements to stay with a friend. The Head looked down at his desk and said gently that it was a pity that she no longer seemed to participate in school affairs. Flaring, she asked whether he was criticising her work and he said no, Eleanor; not your work, your attitude.

'In that case, I think it would be a good idea if I gave in my notice,' she said, and although he left his desk and came across to take her hand, he didn't disagree.

She spent a tormented night, and on the following morning contemplated withdrawing her notice with a letter of apology. Then on the following Sunday, as she lingered aimlessly over a late breakfast, she saw the advertisement for Jackdaw's Cottage.

On the spur of the moment she made an offer, and when her offer was accepted her initial reaction was no more than a grim satisfaction in having burned her boats. She had done well to break the more stupidly sentimental ties with Mo, but beyond that she was too weary to care whether she had made a wise decision or not.

3

There were three framed pictures of Mo at the cottage. The one in the sitting-room was a photograph which showed him dressed in jeans and an anorak with a group of eleven-year-olds on a nature ramble, and the second was a small oil painting done by an artist friend which Eleanor had put in a gold gesso frame and hung over the staircase. The third stood by her bedside table, the enlargement of a snap she herself had taken of him in bathing trunks, sitting on a rock with a long garland of seaweed – *Rhodophyceae,* he always said, call it by its proper name – draped round his shoulders. He was laughing with his head thrown back and the salt spray glittering on his beard and powerful body. He could have been a Triton, and sometimes between waking and sleeping she could hear the happy boom of his laugh echoing like a conch shell blown in some mysterious sea-filled cavern. He was a creature of the salt winds and roaring surf, and she told herself that he had merely freed himself from the stifling littleness of urban life and gone back to where he belonged. Having followed his coffin to the Borough crematorium, the thought comforted her.

She lay looking at the photograph by her bed when she woke up on the following morning. Sunlight flickered through the open window and from under the eaves came the fidgeting of sparrows. *(My sparrows . . .)* She lay relishing the idea of another undisturbed and dreamlike day, then remembered that she had made an appointment to visit the County Records Office. Throwing back the sheet, she hurried to shower and dress.

On the way to the town she thought over the previous day's visit to the Reverend Arthur Parsloe, and told herself not to expect too much from this one either. If country

27

vicars tended towards eccentricity, she had also heard something of the torpor of local government, although to be fair one could hardly expect other people to become over-excited about the history of someone else's house.

She found the office close to the town hall and the brisk click of her heels on the tiled floor seemed to be the only sound within miles. She went straight to the reception desk and told them in a clear and courteous voice that she was the Mrs Millard who had telephoned yesterday to make an appointment to trace the—

With a polite smile the girl behind the desk indicated the *Quiet Please* notice prominently displayed. With a murmured apology Eleanor glanced round the book-lined room and saw a number of people seated at a long table piled with manuscripts and books. Every head was raised in her direction.

Disconcerted, she repeated her request in a whisper and the girl indicated that she should sign the visitors' book before taking her place at the table. 'Mr Seward will be along with your material in a moment,' she whispered.

Trying to walk quietly without actually tiptoeing Eleanor made her way to the table and sat down next to a bald man who made grudging room for her. One by one the heads returned to their labours, and feeling like a schoolgirl elevated to a new class Eleanor removed a notebook and ballpoint from her handbag and placed them neatly in front of her. She then sat gazing out of the opposite window.

Mr Seward proved to be a young man of spidery build, with lank brown hair and anxious eyes. He approached Eleanor with a shy smile to which she responded with no more enthusiasm than good manners dictated. Depositing an armful of books and rolled-up manuscripts in her vicinity he bent close and said in a rapid whisper: 'Mrs Millard? Asham Parva? Sheet number 7 on the Ordnance Survey. . .'

Unrolling the map he placed it in front of her, then peered over her shoulder. 'We'll start by getting you identified. Where are you near?'

'Down a long cart track past Peaslake Farm.'

'Do you know which manor you're in?'

28

'Look, there it is!' Eleanor pounced jubilantly. 'Jack-daw's Cott.' Pride filled her, making her flush slightly.

'Ah yes. Rather hidden away, isn't it?'

'I like it.'

'Yes, of course.' He took a step backwards as if in self-defence. 'Now, what is it exactly that you—'

'I want to trace its history, but most of all I want to know who built it.'

'How old is it?'

'About four hundred years.'

She looked at him expectantly, but instead of appearing awed he murmured something to the effect that it might be difficult. 'Very few people were sufficiently literate to leave written records behind them in those days, but we'll do our best. You've found nothing in the deeds? Have you tried the parish registers? What about manorial rolls?'

He spoke in the same rapid whisper, then indicated a large book near the top of the pile he had brought. 'I think you'd better start with Melville's *Listed Dwellings*, although it may not have anything; then have a look at the section on Asham Parva in Barnard's *Record of County Parishes* – which is this green volume – and if that doesn't give you a lead try Rowbottom & Siddley, which are *those* three. . .'

He tiptoed away. Slowly she reached for the first volume and opened her notebook in readiness, but as he had warned Melville bore no reference to the cottage. Turning to the chapter that dealt with Asham Parva she read care-fully through dry descriptions of the church, the two pubs, the manor house and the site where an old priory had once stood, but that was all.

Barnard's *Record of County Parishes* was more helpful and she became increasingly absorbed by its discursive Victorian style. It had one reference to Jackdaw's Cottage in connection with the non-payment of tithes, and although no names or details were given she found the situation easy to imagine. Engrossed, she returned effortlessly to the role of painstaking student as she noted facts and sifted suppo-sitions, intent now on placing the cottage in the wider context of parish life.

The first volume of Rowbottom & Siddley referred to the discontent expressed in 1712 among poor people in the district of Asham Parva upon being ordered to repair the main turnpike road under the direction of the (nameless) yeoman farmer who dwelt at *Jackdawes,* and for the first time it occurred to her to wonder why the cottage had been named after a bird. Perhaps at one time the place had been planted with the kind of trees that jackdaws like to nest in; then she remembered folk tales in which jackdaws were invariably associated with medieval church towers. . .

She looked up, tapping her pen against her teeth. Through the big window she could see the car park, but her gaze was focused upon two small dry smears in the topmost pane. She stared at them, her thoughts elsewhere, and they stared back at her like a pair of eyes before being extinguished when a member of the staff switched on the overhead lights.

She was startled when Mr Seward came up behind her bearing a roll of parchment tied round with ribbon.

'Just come across this one. Careful, it's rather fragile – dated 1640 I think I'm right in saying.'

He unrolled it. Silently Eleanor helped him, holding down the brittle top edge. It was an original map, the date set in a graceful swirl of penmanship.

'All done by hand,' she whispered reverently.

'Parchment and quill. Now, where are we. . .' He leaned over her shoulder again.

'Asham Magna. . .Asham Parva. . .the church. How tiny the fields were then.'

'Look, there it is.' He pointed. 'In the manor of Bellropes.'

She drew a sharp breath. 'Someone drew the cottage in 1640, and it was just as it is now.'

'And there's the name. Dawes – Jacob Dawes. . .'

She sat staring at the careful little drawing, marvelling at its accuracy. The ink had faded to no more than a pale golden thread and she touched with a loving forefinger the name Jacob Dawes that had been written against the patchwork of little fields.

'It was obviously known as Jacob Dawes' to begin with

and gradually became corrupted to Jackdaws—'

'And Jacob Dawes was the man who built it, wasn't he?' She turned to look at him.

'I think it's probably safe to assume that,' he said. 'At least, in the absence of any sort of proof to the contrary.'

'Jacob Dawes. . .' She let the name fill her mind, then bent over the map again, tracing the curves in the lane and looking for Peaslake Farm, where the Laceys lived.

'I'm awfully sorry,' Mr Seward whispered hoarsely, 'but I'm afraid we're closing for lunch now.'

To her surprise she saw that she was the only person left sitting at the table.

'I didn't realise—' Hastily she helped him to reassemble the books into a pile. They carried them back to his desk and she hesitated for a moment by the door as he switched off the lights and searched in his pocket for the keys.

They walked to the car park together, and when they reached her Fiesta she held out her hand.

'Thank you for discovering Jacob Dawes for me. Somehow it was very important.'

'I was only doing my job, Mrs Millard.' He took her hand and shook it rather awkwardly. 'It sounds a lovely cottage.'

'It is,' she said. Then added on impulse: 'If you like old buildings why don't you come out and see it?'

She was surprised by the pleasure that lit up his eyes. He looked so young and humble that she repeated the invitation. 'Come out one evening and have a drink. I'd be delighted to show you round, in return for all you've done for me.'

'Would Sunday be all right?' He hovered as she unlocked the car door.

'Sunday evening would be fine. Shall we say about eight? And of course, you've got a very good map to show you the way, haven't you?' She laughed up at him through the window.

He stood watching as she drove off, then trudged across the car park to his own battered blue Mini into which he folded himself before making for the open country, in some secluded corner of which he would open his packet of rough-cut sandwiches and drink his flask of coffee.

31

She wished Mo could be there. Although she had bought the place partially as an attempt to compensate for losing him, she often wondered what he would have thought of it. Whether he would have loved its serene beauty and admired the way she had furnished it – a far cry from the old square table and the Woolworths knives and forks – or whether he would have found it pretentious and precious and too far from the thunder of real life.

But whether the cottage appealed to him or not, he would have been very moved and excited by the discovery of Jacob Dawes, for Mo. loved people above all else and Jacob Dawes had been a real person some four hundred years ago.

Jacob Dawes. . . It was as if she had awoken him from a long sleep.

Wandering round the quiet garden before going to bed that night she tried to imagine how the cottage would have looked in his day. New and raw and rough, she supposed, with rushes on the floor and the minimum of furniture. But he would have been very proud of it – as proud as she was now – and it seemed a pity that there was no way of telling him that his cottage was not only still standing, but loved and appreciated.

The scent of the old shrub roses lay heavily on the air, and already she had learned to identify most of them from a book. The Great Maiden's Blush and its sister rose Celeste with its soft pink blooms stood tall and dense on either side of the path that led to the mulberry tree and she turned to look back at the cottage, tracing every curve and angle of its steep roof in the silvery-grey light.

Mo would have loved it. Suddenly she felt certain of it, and wandering on past the glimmering lilies had the impression that he was there somewhere in the garden with her. She believed in neither God nor ghosts, yet found it feasible enough that some indefinable essence should remain of such a vibrant and vital person. Somewhere among the dark bushes she heard the sudden sharp snap of a twig and smiled to herself at the thought of Mo's big blundering feet. She had never known such a combination of clumsy feet and delicate hands, and envisaged him

32

tramping mud over the pale yellow carpets as he brought her some small wild creature cupped tenderly against his chest. Yes, he would have loved it here, and the sleeping garden was full of his presence.

Reluctantly she wandered back to the cottage, watching the moths dance feather-light among the lavender and listening to the shivering cry of an owl across the valley. She went inside, closing and locking the front door for the night, and leaning against the sitting-room wall was too lost in the contemplation of her home to see the face that was watching her through the window.

4

The days passed gracefully, and at five past eight on Sunday evening young Mr Seward arrived, bumping squeakily down the track and stopping the Mini outside the gate. Peering apprehensively from under the brim of a linen sunhat he impressed Eleanor as being no more than nineteen or twenty. Smiling, she went down the narrow flagged path to greet him.

'How very nice to see you!'

'You too, Mrs Millard.' He clutched at her hand and shook it violently. 'It's very nice of you to invite me.'

'Come in,' she said, amused and gratified by the way his eyes darted hungrily at the cottage in the background.

'It's a beauty.' He stepped back towards the gate in order to get a better view. 'That must be the original stack, and the steep pitch of the roof is an immediate indication of its age – and I believe that's the remains of a mullion, isn't it?'

'I don't know,' she said indulgently. 'You tell me.'

He began to walk round the path under the windows while she followed, watching him and listening to each murmured comment with the quiet satisfaction of a loving parent.

'Moulded bressummers. And look there, what lovely curved windbraces under the eaves. In later houses of this sort you'll find that the windbraces are straight. . .'

They stopped at the back of the cottage, close beside the kitchen door where a honeysuckle scrambled almost to the roof, and she continued to watch while his attention turned slowly to the view over the little valley. After another hot day the sky had paled to a faded blue and a lone rook flew homeward, lamenting to itself in a quiet creaking voice. The corn was growing dark against the last flush of sunset and everywhere around them the earth was releasing the sweet damp smell of nightfall.

Without speaking they walked round the garden, following the little paths that twisted between old fruit trees and the high cliffs of roses.

'It was all planted by the people I bought it from,' she said finally. 'I don't know much about gardening yet, but I'm doing a sort of crash course from books – at the moment it doesn't seem to demand much attention apart from watering and a bit of hoeing.'

She showed him the mulberry and the lilies, and then in the rough grass near the hedge that separated the garden from the cornfields, the pond.

'Pity it's dried up,' she said. 'I'd like it to have goldfish and ducks and things.'

'I believe that ducks attack goldfish,' he said deferentially. 'So I think it would have to be one or the other.'

They laughed, and she said what a pity it was that you couldn't have everything in this life.

'I think you've come pretty near to it.'

'I no longer have a husband,' she said gently, and led the way back to the cottage. She took him through the front entrance, determined that he should receive the full impact of the interior. It wasn't lost on him, and he stood on the threshold of the long low sitting-room with its honey-gold timbers and huge open fireplace banked with flowers.

'Come along in,' she said. 'Sit down, and tell me what you'd like to drink.'

He came slowly across the lemon-coloured carpet, looking about him and squeezing his hat between both hands as if he were wringing it out.

'Just look at that wonderful studwork. It's so uniform

34

and so close together.'

'Studwork?' She looked at him brightly, one hand on hip.

'The upright beams are called studs and that long horizontal one running along the top is a bressummer. All these old timber-framed houses were built to a carefully worked-out pattern, and every piece of wood used in them had its own name according to its function. Thank you,' he added, 'I'd like a small sherry.'

She handed it to him, half expecting that he would have asked for a coke. His extreme youthfulness still daunted her a little, and in an effort to ignore it she raised her own glass and proposed a toast to Jacob Dawes.

'Jacob Dawes,' he repeated, then added diffidently: 'And here's to the lady who lives in the house that he built.'

'The house that Jake built. . .'

They sipped, and young Mr Seward placed his carefully wrung-out sunhat on the floor by the side of his chair while Eleanor seated herself opposite him.

'What would he have been like?' she asked suddenly. 'Working on historical supposition, I mean.'

'Jacob? Well now, let's see.' He took another small sip, then sat further back in the chair. 'From the size of the place he would most likely have been a yeoman freeholder with perhaps a cow, almost certainly a pig or two, and a few sheep – don't forget that the wool trade, although past its medieval peak, was still flourishing in this area – and for the rest, I think he'd be practising what they call subsistence agriculture. He'd be hardworking – up at dawn, bed at dusk except on special occasions – and building this house with his own two hands was his personal expression of sanguinity.' He was regaining some of the confidence he had shown among the documents in the Record Office.

'Go on,' she said.

'I'm not boring you?'

'Oh, please, Mr—'

'Could you call me Eric?'

'Please, Eric, tell me some more.'

'Well. . .when I say building this house with his own two hands, he would have had some help of course. Someone

35

in his little circle of family or friends would probably have been a sawyer, for instance, and all the main timbers would have been pit-sawn, then carefully numbered and brought up to the site. They'd fit them together, using mortise and tenon joints, and then with all the help they could get they'd pull the skeleton of the thing upright with ropes and chains.'

'I can visualise it staggering to its feet like a new-born foal,' said Eleanor, greatly moved.

'After that, Jacob would have infilled between the timbers with wattle and daub, then finished the walls off with a thin coat of plaster made from lime, sand and cowhair—'

'Cowhair?'

'It was very supple, and resistant to weather changes. But of course you mustn't imagine that it was all that sophisticated as a dwelling.' He looked at her with a touch of severity. 'It must have been a mere four walls, a roof, and a beaten earth floor.'

She got up to pour a little more sherry. 'Uncomfortable, to say the least.'

'Not by their standards. Thank you – ' He took the glass from her. 'Because they must have been a pretty tough bunch.'

They sat silent, relaxed and companionable. Daylight had drained from the sky and through the open window came the quiet rustle of leaves, as if some small nocturnal creature were rummaging its way through the garden.

'But I don't think they could have been all that different from us,' he went on. 'They must have loved and hated, laughed and wept – probably the main difference between us and them is our comparative lack of fear. We know so much more than they did.'

'Sometimes the things I know make me feel very frightened indeed,' Eleanor said. Reaching out, she switched on the lamp by her chair. 'There are lots of things I wish I didn't know.'

'But nothing can be as frightening as sheer brute ignorance.'

'And as a teacher I ought to be aware of that.'

He sat looking at her with frank curiosity. 'What made you come to live here?'

'It depends in what sense you mean. In one way I came to live here because I saw the cottage advertised in the press and bought it. But I also came because I'd come to the end of doing what I did before, and I knew that ultimately I'd have to begin a new chapter somewhere else. My husband and I were both teachers and after he died I didn't seem to have anything left to give. I needed to be in some kind of no man's land before I came to a decision about the future.'

'Oh dear. I'm sorry. . .'

'Don't be. I had so much happiness.'

'So – so how long will you stay here like this?'

'I hope I'll always stay here,' she replied, 'but it won't always be like this. My days as a lady of leisure are strictly limited for financial reasons, and I hope that before long I'll be ready to face the outside world again. I expect I'll go back to teaching, maybe in a local school.'

'I get the impression that you're a very good teacher,' he said, 'so don't hide yourself away for too long.'

The rustling in the garden had ceased. Apart from their quiet voices there was no sound.

'Strange,' he said, looking at the wall behind her head. 'Shadows moving in a deep silence.'

'I thought shadows always were silent.'

'Yes, but whatever makes them rarely is. Wind in the trees, a fluttering bird, footsteps—'

'Your job has given you a taste for the supernatural,' she said smilingly. Suddenly aware that she was enjoying his company she topped up their glasses again before inviting him to look over the rest of the cottage.

She showed him the kitchen, the dining-room, the two spare bedrooms and the bathroom, and then, aware that her intentions might be misconstrued, opened her own bedroom door and said dismissively: 'Oh, and that's my room—' as she walked away down the passage.

He followed behind, and although he made no comment on the crisp and beautiful simplicity of the furnishings, he stopped every now and then to touch with sensitive fingers the curve of a timber or a window that still bore the traces of an original sliding shutter.

'Oh Lord,' he said finally, 'I do wish we could get into the roof. It's the roof that tells you the real story and I wouldn't mind betting that this one's got a king-post.'

'Is that good?'

For some reason he began to laugh, a convulsive hic-coughing sound as if he were out of practice. 'Very good indeed.'

'So why are you laughing?' By this time she was laughing too.

'It must be because I'm enjoying myself.'

The simple statement had the effect of sobering them both. 'I'm sorry,' she said, 'but I don't think there's any sort of trap-door into the roof,' and led the way downstairs again.

Outside the sitting-room he paused. 'No really, I must go. It's getting late and they might be wondering where I am.'

'Who's they?'

'My wife and children.'

'Oh,' she said blankly, then in order to cover her surprise, added: 'I wish I'd realised – your wife must think me very discourteous not to have included her.'

He gave a small pained smile. 'I don't think she could have managed it. She's fairly busy most of the time.'

'How many children have you got?' Moving towards the front door she was increasingly surprised by the thought of him in the role of husband and father.

'Two. One is five and the other nearly seven.'

He stood by her side as she opened the door. Light flooded the pathway and picked out the motionless shapes of the roses.

'Such a warm still night,' she said uselessly. 'I wish we could have some rain.'

'Should be a good harvest.' He stood staring up at the dark purple sky with its dusting of stars, then drew a deep breath and said goodbye.

'I loved the cottage and I so enjoyed your hospitality.'

'Thank you for coming, Eric, and don't forget to bring your wife next time.'

'I will – I will . . .' He shook her outstretched hand with the same violent pumping action. 'Thank you very much, Mrs Millard. . .'

She watched him hurry to the gate and then blend with the heavy shadows out in the lane. Although the outside lamp was switched on its beam didn't reach him and she wondered if she should have accompanied him to the car with a torch. A moment later she heard the engine start.

She stood thinking over his visit and watching how the shadows down by the gate seemed to move and sway and merge into one another. As he had said, it was strange that shadows should move so silently and on such a still, windless night. Staring hard at them she realised with a slight quickening of the pulse that she couldn't tell what they were the shadows of. How little one knew about anything. The furtive silence that covered the garden was probably hiding a thousand small creatures who watched and waited, all bound by the same cruel law of eat or be eaten. They were probably watching her, too; willing her, the alien daytime creature, to go back inside her box and leave the darkness to those who understood it.

Yet something made her linger. The scent of the roses and lilies, the languid dance of a moth against the lamp and a strange feeling that Mo was near. A lot of the anguish and bitterness of losing him had faded since she came to the cottage – she had only once woken up in tears after dreaming about him, whereas at the flat it had been an almost nightly occurrence – and during the past week or so she had found herself able to catch sight of his photograph suddenly without a stab of pain. The thing was healing, mellowing into something she could come to terms with, and standing outside the cottage on that warm velvet night she told herself that the more she was at peace with herself, the closer Mo would be to her. He would be close, but not of course in any way gruesomely so, and she would continue to live neatly among the lovely possessions she had accumulated, indirectly because of him.

Smiling, she went inside and closed the door, and the golden lamplight illuminated her like a character in a stage set for the face that was watching through the window.

It was too early to go to bed, and in any case she wasn't tired. Switching on the portable radio she listened to a programme about the Lebanon for a few minutes, then switched it off. Taking the two empty sherry glasses through to the kitchen she noticed that Eric Seward had left his hat down by the side of his chair. The hat looked a little grubby inside and she thrust it into the small cupboard where she kept her gardening gloves.

She washed the glasses and polished them dry, then wondered whether she would like a cheese sandwich. She thought about it earnestly, standing there in the kitchen with the refrigerator making a soft background noise, and then decided that she wasn't really hungry. She might make some coffee, but not just yet. She went back to the sitting-room, drawing the curtains and then settling down with a new book about roses.

Once you have surrendered yourself to the romance of the old shrub roses you will never willingly break free. Their names alone weave a magic spell – bourbon, musk and damask, the gallicas and centifolias, all of them carrying us back on the perfumed mists of time. . .

A soft tapping broke the silence. Sharply she raised her head and sat listening. It seemed to come from the front door, and when it stopped she remained motionless, mystified but not afraid. She waited for several minutes but the noise was not repeated and she returned to her book.

Then the front door clicked and she heard the slow creak of its hinges. She stood up with a gasp, her book flying, and realised almost instantly that it was Eric Seward calling back to retrieve his hat.

'Eric?'

Swiftly she went through to the little hallway and then

halted abruptly, her hands clasped. A man was standing in the open doorway, his eyes huge with an unspeakable terror.

They seemed to stand staring at one another for a long while, each waiting for the other to move first, yet she could take in no more than a confused impression of a shortish, rather stockily built man wearing a brown shirt over pants of the same colour. She had never seen him before.

'Who are you?' she demanded in a sudden shrill voice. 'What do you want?'

The man seemed to make some attempt to speak, but failed. She saw his eyes flick a quick glance behind her, then return to her face as if mesmerised. She had the impression that given the power of movement he would have made a bolt for it.

'What are you doing here?'

He swallowed convulsively. 'I – I know not –'

'Then I suggest you go back to where you came from before I ring for the police,' she said tartly. She took a step forward, intending to close the door on him, then stopped hastily as the man gave a small terrified cry and cringed back against the doorpost, covering his head with his hands.

Something about him began to fill her with a new, strange kind of fear. Already it had crossed her mind that he was a gypsy or a vagrant of some kind, but forcing herself to study his appearance in greater detail, something told her that his identity was far more extraordinary than that. She saw now that his rough brown shirt was belted at the waist and that he was wearing some kind of breeches stuffed into the tops of knee-length stockings. With his thick bob of dark hair and cowering demeanour he could have been a Russian serf escaped from the pages of Dostoevsky.

Making a huge effort to speak calmly she said: 'Look, I don't know who you are or what you want, but you must go away from here. I can't help you and I have nothing to give you.'

Slowly the man uncovered his head. He took a step forward and to her added horror fell on his knees.

41

'I know not what's to do with me – how I come here. . .'
He had a country voice, the accent not unlike the ones she
had heard at the Laceys' farm.

'Get up,' she said sharply.

'In God's name, mistress,' he said, 'help me.'

She closed her eyes, then opened them again and said as
slowly and patiently as possible: 'Who are you? Tell me
who you *are*.'

'I know not—'

'But what is your name? What do people call you?' Even
as she spoke the words she became aware of an insane
suspicion.

Still on his knees the man looked up at her imploringly.
'My name is Jacob Dawes, mistress.'

She tried to enunciate, and failed. 'This is a joke,' she
managed to say finally. 'Someone's playing a joke. . .'

The man stood up. 'My name is Jacob Dawes,' he repeated. 'Son of John Dawes and his wife Eliza and I know
not how I came to be here.'

'Then I'll tell you,' she said. 'Your friend Eric Seward
thought it would be a good joke to get you to dress up and
play a trick on me. You probably left your car down the
lane and walked the last two hundred yards, and then—'
Her voice died as the man's expression of utter incomprehension endorsed her own disbelief in the idea. 'One of us
is mad,' she said, then added suddenly: 'Where did Jacob
Dawes live?'

'Along of his mother and father until he were wed, then
he built his own dwelling.' The man ventured another
glance at his surroundings and she could have sworn that
the perplexity in his eyes was genuine. 'This seemed like
the place we set it down in, and outsides it seemed like my
dwelling place, but it's all of a turnabout in here.'

'You really believe that you're Jacob Dawes?'

'Who else then might I be?'

She began to laugh, the sound ringing with hysteria. 'In
that case you're a ghost – a figment of my imagination – if I
tried to touch you you'd disappear!'

She stretched out her hand, and straining every nerve the
man contrived to remain motionless.

'Oh, my God. . .'

Her laughter died as her fingers encountered the rough wool of his shirt, the cool leather of his belt and then finally the living warmth of his hand. She took his hand in hers, noting the harshness of its skin, the hard bluntness of its fingernails and, in spite of its implied strength, the way that it trembled.

'You're real,' she whispered. 'Which can only mean that you're some sort of imposter, unless. . .'

'And who might you be?' His fingers began to flex within her grasp and it seemed as if his fear was melting into a sense of baffled astonishment to equal her own.

'My name is Eleanor Millard and I bought this cottage earlier in the year.'

'What year?'

'1981.'

'19—' He shook his hand free and turned away.

'But do you know the name of the place? It's called Jackdaw's Cottage and its name is derived from—' she hesitated for a moment, 'from yours.'

He stood looking at the wall without speaking.

'Jacob Dawes,' she said. 'Tell me what's happened.'

'It's Satan's work. I want no part of it.'

'Unless this *is* some kind of elaborate hoax on someone's part, it would seem that you haven't got much choice.'

'You reckon I'm dead, then?'

Helplessly she shook her head. 'I don't know. How can you be – and be like you are?'

'Answer me one riddle, then,' he said, turning to face her again. 'How can it be darkness without and yet daylight within?'

'By means of electricity.' She watched him very carefully as she spoke, testing his expression for the slightest hint of duplicity, but there was none. She could have sworn that this was a human being as worried and as deeply apprehensive as she.

'I can't explain this any more than you can,' she said finally, 'but you must understand that I've no wish to harm you. If you really and honestly are Jacob Dawes and you've fallen through some sort of – of weird hole in time, then

43

you'd better come in. After all, it was your home once.'

Watching her with all the wariness of a wild creature he sidled after her into the sitting-room.

'Sit down.'

He remained standing, his hands hanging and his eyes measuring the distance to the door. Seating herself, she bravely attempted a smile of encouragement.

'You built this house, didn't you? Somewhere about 1580, I believe.'

'I have no recollection of the year, mistress. But it were almost a twelvemonth after they burnt the priory.'

'Who burnt it?'

'Why, the soldiers did. Because of the Jesuits who lay sheltered there, and because it was known that the Pope blessed the Armada.'

'Good God. . .' Eleanor said helplessly.

He was extraordinarily convincing. So much so that her fear was increasingly giving way to a passionate interest. Grimacing, she told herself that her one aim should be to find out all she could from him before she woke up.

'Jacob, tell me about yourself. Tell me what it was like when you lived here.'

He took her literally. 'It was a fair-sized dwelling then, and not portioned off. All this wealth of chattels makes my head ring—'

'It's bound to be different,' she said with quick sympathy. 'Four hundred years is a long time, and it's a miracle that your house is still standing, but only this evening a man who is an expert on historical houses – houses like yours, I mean – was looking round it and admiring the way you had built it—'

She stopped when she saw his confusion. It was obvious that he couldn't follow her rapid modern speech. 'I was just telling you,' she said very slowly, as if to a foreigner, 'that my generation of people loves and admires the houses you built. We think you were very skilful and very practical.'

'I never built more than the one,' he said.

'But it's such a beautiful little house, Jacob,' she said eagerly. 'I came here from a city of houses that my generation of people has built and they are ugly – very, very ugly –

44

and when I saw this one I felt so happy and at peace—'

'There is no weather within?' He looked up at the ceiling and she realised what he meant.

'No, no, the rain doesn't come in. Neither does the wind. . .'

'That is well,' he said, and smiled at her for the first time.

It was an unexpectedly humorous smile, and she was now sufficiently relaxed to study him in detail. His thick bob of dark hair framed a face difficult to put an age to; the eyes seemed young in their darting brightness but his skin was dry and rather creased and his teeth looked to her to be in the process of decay. It was a strong, rather obdurate face with its straight fleshy nose and short upper lip, and this time he didn't flinch when she put out her hand to touch him.

I must wake up now, she thought. It's gone on for long enough, because I know that people who are dead can only regain reality in someone else's dream. Yet she had never felt more awake or more rationally aware of what was happening. There was none of the flickering, time-jumping quality of a dream – she could even hear her own wrist-watch ticking – and it occurred to her that the only way she could prove the reality of the situation would be to walk upstairs and see whether or not she was lying asleep in bed.

'Mistress,' the man standing in front of her shifted uneasily, 'my good wife waits without.'

'Your *wife?*' Filled with sudden delight, she no longer cared about the problem of reality. 'Oh, good heavens – bring her in!'

She stood with her hands clasped, watching as he went to the door and peered out. She heard him speaking softly, putting out his hand as if to encourage someone, and after a moment or two she saw a small bowed figure, entirely obscured by a hooded cloak, creep over the threshold. He brought it gently into the room and stood with it in front of Eleanor.

'This is my good wife, Mary.'

Sensing a timidity far greater even than that of Jacob, Eleanor remained motionless.

'Welcome home, Mary,' she said quietly.

45

The figure seemed to bend a little closer towards the floor in an agony of suppressed fear. Its head was still closely shrouded by the hood, and Eleanor caught the faint sound of quick, uneven breathing.

'Come, woman,' Jacob said, and attempted to uncover her head. There was a fleeting glimpse of fair hair, then a small hand came out from the interior of the cloak and dragged the hood back in place again. Catching Eleanor's eye Jacob winked, and she found herself taking note of the fact that people had obviously employed the same silent mode of expression in the reign of Elizabeth Tudor. It seemed more and more as if she were awake and not dreaming.

'How do you do, Mary Dawes,' she said in the same quiet voice. 'Please don't be afraid of me. I'm the woman who lives in your house now and I want you to know that I love and cherish it, and that I have often thought about you and wondered what you were like. Will you be friends with me, Mary?'

She held out her hand. There was a slight movement under the cloak but nothing more.

'The mistress wishes you well,' Jacob said. 'Give her your hand on it.'

Reluctantly the hand came out from the heavy woollen folds. It felt human but very cold, and Eleanor took it between both of her own and tried to press warmth and encouragement into it.

'Mary,' she said. 'I'm so glad you've come back.'

'The youngest wench of John Todd, the wheelwright over Great Chiddingford way,' Jacob said, and pushed the hood so that it fell back irretrievably over the woman's shoulders. She sank to the floor and began to sob.

'Lord have mercy. . .Christ have mercy upon us. . .'

'There's no harm here,' Jacob said, hauling her upright again and supporting her. 'See, there's no harm. The mistress is kindly disposed. Speak to the mistress, Mary—'

Covering her face with her hands Mary dropped a hasty curtsy then cringed back against him. Compared to his wife Jacob now seemed tolerably at ease, and he led her to the sofa that stood opposite the great fireplace. Together they

46

sat down on the edge of it.

Slowly and very quietly Eleanor moved to the drinks table and poured three glasses of sherry. She went over to the sofa with a glass in either hand.

'Jacob and Mary,' she said, offering them. 'I think we ought to drink a toast.'

Jacob accepted one while Mary hid her face in his shoulder. Smiling sympathetically Eleanor put the second glass on a small stool close at hand then went back to the table for her own.

'Jacob and Mary Dawes,' she said, raising it. 'I drink a toast to you, and to the house that you built.'

And I'm not dreaming, she thought, watching as Jacob took first a cautious sip and then a larger one. Nothing in my life has ever been more vivid and positive than this. These two people are living entities, and so am I. All three of us are equally real and I refuse to search for explanations.

She saw Jacob offer his glass to Mary, who cringed further back into the shadows before surreptitiously taking a tiny sip.

'And you will not betray us to the clergy, mistress?' Jacob gave Eleanor a sudden sharp glance.

'The clergy? Of course not – why?'

'Because this is a business of the spirit and they would see fit to bring down the wrath of Almighty God on our heads. They would punish us for meddlesome wickedness—' he replaced his arm round Mary as she gave an involuntary cry of fear, 'but we have done no evil.'

'Of course you haven't.' Eleanor continued to speak slowly, giving each word its full weight. 'I know that you are both good people.'

'We walk in the way of the Lord.'

'Of course you do. It's quite obvious that you are no more to blame for what's happened than I am, and I will see to it that nothing harms you so long as you are in my care.'

'How long shall we bide here?'

'I don't know. I think we'll just have to wait and see.'

'But what will become of us if— '

'Don't worry, Jacob,' she said. 'I've got a feeling that

47

everything is going to be all right.'

Strange words to say to a couple of ghosts, she thought. For, ignoring their apparent solidity, what else could they possibly be? Yet in spite of the almost unbelievable situation in which she found herself, she realised that she was becoming steadily more accustomed to it. Excitement was taking the place of fear and she was now almost on the point of accepting their presence with or without a rational explanation.

She finished her sherry and then said briskly: 'Now, first of all I want to warn you about the light.' She pointed to the lamp. 'It can appear and disappear very quickly, but I promise that it won't harm you.'

For a moment Jacob looked at her uncomprehendingly, then he nodded.

'Hold my hand, woman,' he said, 'for we are about to see a miracle.'

The tiny click might have been a rifle shot, and when the lamplight was extinguished and then just as suddenly restored, Mary hid her eyes in her husband's shoulder with a gasp of terror.

'See – open your eyes –' he prised her head away, 'there is nothing to fear. Only a wonderful miracle that the mistress had wrought to roll back the darkness...'

Seen clearly for the first time, the woman's face was small and drained of colour, the skin stretched tightly over delicate bones. Her hair, which was a pale gold, was pulled back from her forehead and disappeared somewhere beneath the neck of her cloak. She was rather beautiful in a strange, sad sort of way, and whenever she dared to raise her eyes Eleanor saw that they were very large and still dazed with fear.

'And now, I think it's time for you both to see over the rest of the house,' she told them, and smilingly held out her hands. Jacob stood up with alacrity while Mary clung to him in silence.

Slowly Eleanor led the way through the rooms for the second time that evening, and if Eric Seward's admiration had given her pleasure, the awed amazement of the original owners filled her with a rich glow of philanthropic delight.

'I suppose the kitchen must show the most revolutionary change since your time here,' she said. The bright lighting made them flinch, but when she invited Jacob to switch it off and on for himself he did so with an exclamation of triumph.

'Nowadays we cook by electricity – that thing is called a hob unit, and over there is the oven where we roast meat and bake cakes – and look, Mary, this big square thing with a round hole in the front is a machine that does all the washing. It washes all the clothes and the sheets – all you have to do is to put them inside and then switch it on – electricity again, you see. . .'

They followed her round, gravely attentive but comprehending no more than a tenth of the things she told them.

'All this is called technology,' she said, 'and today some of us are worried that it is all becoming too important in our lives. We feel that we may be in danger of forgetting how to do the simpler things for ourselves. In some ways I agree with this, but on the other hand I can't really see any particular virtue in performing hard and unpleasant tasks oneself merely for the sake of doing so. But I do think that we ought to show appreciation of our freedom by giving more time and thought to the creation and preservation of beautiful things. Don't you agree?'

Standing close together they nodded obediently.

'And to me,' went on Eleanor, 'one of the most beautiful things I have ever encountered is your house. No technology on earth could reproduce it – to begin with, it would cut all the beams straight and uniform! – and when I bought it I felt right from the start that I had taken on some kind of special *trust* to care for it, not only because of its actual beauty but as a sort of humble tribute to you people who first created it.'

She led them upstairs and they reeled back from their reflections in the full length bathroom mirror. When they had recovered she showed them how the lavatory worked, and their astonishment to see hot water gushing out of the bath tap brought a sudden haze of emotional tears to her eyes. She had rarely been similarly affected by her pupils.

And there was no longer any question of fear on her part;

49

she no longer cared whether they were ghosts or a dream – (she was *not* lying asleep in her bed when she showed them her room) – because it now seemed as if this was what she had been waiting for. The shadows in the garden, the snapping of twigs and the feeling of another presence close by had been nothing to do with poor Mo, but it had been everything to do with Jacob Dawes. The rediscovery of his name on the old map in the Record Office had made him stir in his long sleep, and she was convinced now that her passionate interest had somehow had the power to revive both him and his wife.

Lovingly she led them downstairs again. 'You must be hungry – I know *I* am, after all this excitement! – so let's cook some bacon and eggs.'

Bustling them into the kitchen again she was too busy rummaging in the fridge to notice Mary pulling at Jacob's sleeve, but when she turned to face them she saw Mary whispering close to his ear.

'What does she want, Jacob?'

'The woman frets about the baby. 'Tis only a nursling—'

'A *baby*?' cried Eleanor, overjoyed. 'Oh, bring him in – why on earth did you leave him outside?'

She hastened with them through to the hall and then stood with Mary as Jacob opened the door.

The outside lamp was still on, and its circle of silvery moth-speckled light illuminated the upturned faces of a group of children. They were standing close together, in silence, and an older girl with long pale hair was holding a tightly swaddled bundle in her arms.

'Are these—?' began Eleanor faintly.

'Eleven children, mistress,' Jacob said. 'Six living and five dead, three in infancy, and two of the sweating sickness.'

She tried to smile, but her lips suddenly felt a little dry and stiff.

'Well, well,' she said at last, 'you'd all better come in, hadn't you?'

6

Eric Seward walked into the dining-room and closed the door. It was a small untidy room seldom used for dining and now regarded by him as a study and a place of refuge. The sideboard was piled with books and on the table stood a typewriter surrounded by a sea of miscellaneous papers.

He seated himself and gazed forlornly at the green folder containing the first chapter of a book he intended to write on the social influence of the squire magistrate, and then reached for a blank sheet of paper and began to write a letter.

Dear Mrs Millard, I have just returned home from my visit to you and feel that I must express my thanks for such a very pleasant evening. I think your cottage is delightful, and whether or not you actually master-minded its restoration doesn't really matter; sufficient to say that your affectionate sensitivity in relation to historical buildings is immediately apparent to any outsider. And even more striking than the visual aspect is the tranquil atmosphere – I couldn't help feeling that you have somehow banished all the stress and ugliness of modern life and substituted a sort of timeless peace. You and Jackdaw's Cottage (or should I now say Jacob Dawes' cottage?) go hand in hand; you belong to one another, and I wish you many happy years . . .

The door opened and his wife appeared.
'How long have you been back?'
'About an hour.'
'Where were you?'
'Does it matter?'
Corinne Seward came into the room and perched herself

51

on the edge of the table, swinging her legs. She had been unusually pretty when they married, but now at twenty-eight the tender lines of her face were hardening into a thin, mean look. She had a lot of frizzily curled hair worn in a low thicket-like fringe through which she stared at Seward like an accusatory poodle.

He sighed, and unobtrusively covered his half-written letter with his sleeve. 'I was looking over an old house.'

'Well, if you can't make it with human beings or animals I suppose houses are the next best thing. Pity you didn't get married to a pile of bricks and mortar.'

She got off the table and rambled restlessly round the room. She was wearing a crumpled cotton smock and jeans and the faint, not unpleasant smell of marijuana emanated from her as she passed.

'It didn't occur to you that I was going out?'

'My not being here doesn't generally stop you.'

'Can you wonder, trying to live with an egotistical bastard like you? I'd never go anywhere.'

'Well, all right,' he said. 'Here I am, so *go*.'

'I'm not going now. It's too late.'

'It can't be. Your things never start before midnight.'

'Oh, shut up,' she said, and went out banging the door.

He returned to his letter. From the room above his head came the muffled sounds of a child starting to grizzle.

. . . and I wish you many happy years of peace and tranquillity. Perhaps I may be permitted to call again one day – I don't know whether I told you incidentally that the Record Office is planning an exhibition of household account books dating between the years 1600 and 1750, which I think might be of interest to you. In which case I could bring you a ticket to save you the bother

He stopped, and read over the letter as far as it went. Sickened by its note of coy fulsomeness he tore it up and flung the bits into the cardboard box that served as a waste paper basket. Upstairs the grizzling grew louder, and he told himself that the sooner he forgot all about Eleanor Millard and her beautiful timeless peace the better.

II
THE FAMILY

1

Lying in bed at the cottage Eleanor stared into the thin summer darkness and thought with mounting incredulity of what had happened.

The apparent return of Jacob Dawes with wife and family was – well, God knows what it was, her brain was exhausted with the effort of trying to understand – but now her chief amazement was reserved for her own behaviour. How could she have come to accept their appearance with such calm? After the first five minutes or so her fear had diminished and she had been conscious only of a sense of excitement and pleasure.

She must have gone mad. Yes, that was it, she had literally gone mad. She sat up in bed with a jerk, clasping her hands round her knees. The strain of Mo's illness and death, the miserable period which followed and then the relaxing into a state of quiet contentment were all the classic ingredients for a nervous breakdown, and now she was hallucinating. It had been developing for several days, this strange impression of another presence in and around the cottage, and at first she had taken it merely as a strong loving memory of Mo. It was only a matter of chance – some queer flick of a sick brain mechanism – that finally produced Jacob Dawes and not Mo as a living being.

But a living being to her, and to her alone. For she had got to realise that she was ill, and therein lay the explanation. It was the only possible way of solving the otherwise insoluble mystery of how a man and his family had reappeared in flesh and blood form after having been dead for almost four centuries.

I am mad, she thought, and immediately felt a little calmer. That's the explanation, I'm having a nervous breakdown which has resulted in temporary insanity and first thing tomorrow I will make an appointment to see a doctor. There must be one in the village and he will send me to see a specialist, who will prescribe a course of drugs or some psycho-analysis or even group therapy with other people who are suffering from the same sort of thing. We are living in an age of stress but never mind, medical science is keeping up with it and these days we understand so much more about the complexities of the human brain. I'm mad now, but tomorrow I will seek help and within a very short time I will be cured . . .

She lay down again, and was on the point of dozing off when another thought jabbed her back to consciousness. People who thought they were mad never were. They were always proved to be sane, whereas those who most vehemently protested their sanity were the ones often proved wrong.

The darkness wasn't deep enough to conceal the outline of the furniture, merely sufficient to transform it into alien and hostile shapes. Although the window was wide open the air seemed peculiarly hot and sticky and the whine of a solitary mosquito began to scratch at her nerves.

My nerves, she thought, it's all my nerves, then on impulse pushed back the sheet and got out of bed. The illuminated bedside clock showed that it was still only four-thirty, and she stood listening intently for any slight sound that might confirm the presence of Jacob and his family. After giving them all a supper of eggs and bacon and bread and butter she had shown them to the two guest rooms, fetching additional cushions and blankets and spreading them on the floor for the younger children before bidding them all good night. And her principal concern had been that they should sleep secure in the knowledge that while they were under her care no harm would come to them.

She could hear nothing. The cottage seemed to be wrapped in a deathlike silence that nothing would ever break. Even the mosquito was inaudible. She moved over to the door and opened it cautiously, blinking through the dim grey light at the two guest room doors further along the corridor. They were closed, and although she told herself to go along and open them and see what lay behind them - that even if she saw quite clearly the beds and floors littered with the inert forms of sleeping people they would only be figments of her imagination – she hadn't the courage.

Instead she tiptoed down the staircase where the portrait of Mo glimmered faintly and the scent of cut roses mingled with a faint remaining whiff of bacon.

She moved like a sleepwalker, threading her way between the furniture without appearing to notice it. She went into the kitchen for a glass of water then carried it back to the sitting-room and sat down on the sofa before drinking it. Placing the empty glass on the wine table nearby, her bare arm brushed against something made of a heavy rough material. She seized it, frowning and peering at it in the gloom before dropping it on the floor with a muffled cry. It was the cloak that Mary Dawes had been wearing.

She sat staring at the dark shape of it on the sea of pale nylon carpet and telling herself that it wasn't real. That some of the most real-seeming things in the world were only imaginary if you happened to be mentally ill. After a moment or two she bent forward and took a handful of it, crushing it hard in her fingers and then laying it flat on her knee and stroking it with her eyes closed. It was a coarsely woven wool with little irregular knobbles here and there, and when she held it close to her face it had a strange far-off kind of scent that reminded her of herbs and old damp churches.

She stood up and forced herself to put it on. Although it only reached to mid-calf the weight of it seemed considerable and she remained standing there, very tall and straight, staring across the room and thinking: This is not real. This is all part of an illness, a phantom in my mind.

But it didn't seem like it. The cloak as she slowly removed it from her shoulders and draped it tidily across the arm of the sofa was as real and as matter-of-fact as her own tweed winter coat which hung in the cupboard upstairs.

The dead grey light was taking on a luminous edge as she crept upstairs again, and she was halfway to her bedroom when the raucous sound of a man coughing made her start convulsively. Before she could gain the safety of her own room the first of the two guest room doors opened and Jacob Dawes appeared. Crumpled and tousled in the same clothes that he had worn the night before, he bowed to her energetically and said good morning.

'Good morning, Jacob.'

With a little rush she reached her bedroom and was in the act of closing the door by the time he drew level. She sensed his eyes taking in the frilly prettiness of her nightgown.

'So, what's to do, mistress? If it please you I'll lend a hand with the milking.'

There seemed little trace of last night's fear in his voice and she paused confusedly, suddenly realising that she was squinting without her contact lenses.

'Oh no – it's quite all right . . . later on, perhaps . . . '

She closed the door in his face and leaned her back hard against it.

'But 'tis milking time surely—'

'Jacob, I haven't got a cow.'

'No *cow*, mistress?' From the other side of the door his voice sounded full of astonishment. She began to laugh helplessly. Taking her hand off the doorknob she wiped her hair back from her forehead. Tears gathered in her eyes.

'No, Jacob, no cow,' she cried. 'In 1981 all the milk comes out of bottles—'

If he made any reply she didn't hear it. Gulping and whispering to herself *I am ill – I am ill –* she left the door and dressed swiftly in a cotton skirt and blouse. Gliding into the bathroom, which appeared empty and undisturbed, she washed her hands and face, combed her hair and dabbed hastily at her nose with a little make-up.

When she arrived downstairs they were all standing there in the sitting-room, lined up in what seemed like some sort of incredible guard of honour. Jacob stood at the head of it, with Mary next to him and the six children – the eldest girl holding the baby – ranged in order of size. At least, no more of them had appeared like mushrooms during the night; there was no sign of grandparents or uncles and aunts . . .

She said good morning, and Mary and the girls responded by twitching their long skirts in a curtsy while the two big boys touched their foreheads and bowed to her.

Then they all stood looking at her again, waiting politely for the next move.

She stared back at them, standing on the bottom stair with her hand on the baluster, mesmerised by the sheer irrefutable reality of them. In the rapidly strengthening light she took careful, clinical note of the moist freshness of their eyes – brown, save for those of Mary and the eldest girl, which were grey-blue – the faint scent of herbs and old churches that came from them and the stubble that had lengthened on Jacob's chin since the previous evening. She could see them breathing: watch the gentle rise and fall of their breasts, and when one of the smaller children began surreptitiously to scratch its funny-bone she knew perfectly well that she wasn't mad. Somehow the inexplicable had occurred, and when the first hesitant finger of early morning sun touched Mary Dawes' fair hair and brought it to quivering, shining life she knew finally and irrevocably that she was content to accept them as living creatures who had returned from the dead.

'Right,' she said, clapping her hands and smiling briskly, 'first things first. Breakfast in the kitchen for the children and we three will eat in the dining-room. And incidentally, as I haven't got a cow to milk I would mention that I don't normally get up at five o'clock in the morning . . .'

She took a large sliced loaf from the deep freeze which she made into toast. She warmed a pan of milk for the children. ('Look, these are the bottles of milk that a dairy delivers every day to Peaslake Farm. I collect it from the farmer's wife, whose name is Mrs Lacey . . .') She gave the children bowls of cornflakes and gently corrected them when they ate them with their fingers instead of using the spoons she had provided. She made a pot of coffee, and pretended not to notice when Jacob and Mary suppressed a shudder at the strange taste of it. But they ate a good many slices of toast spread with butter and honey and when the baby began to cry the eldest girl brought it to its mother, who unfastened the bodice of her long stuff dress and began to breast-feed it.

It became apparent to Eleanor that the sooner she went to the supermarket the better.

59

'Jacob and Mary,' she said, getting up from the dining table. 'Would you like to come shopping with me?'

They looked at her in perplexity, then Mary returned to watching the baby at work.

'Shopping – going to the market,' persisted Eleanor, and Jacob grinned immediate acceptance.

'We need more food, and perhaps one or two other things as well. Do you think the children would stay quietly at home while we're away?'

'They will do as they are bid.'

'Because, you see, I don't think we could get them all in the car.'

'Car, mistress?'

'That's right,' she said, smiling. 'You've got another big surprise ahead of you.'

The eldest girl's name was Dorcas, and Eleanor gathered that she was about twelve years old. She stood with her hands folded and her head bent respectfully when Eleanor spoke to her.

'Now, Dorcas, I am taking your mother and father with me to buy some food, but we will be gone for only a short while. You will be perfectly safe here, and there is nothing to be afraid of. Perhaps while we are away you will fold the blankets tidily in your rooms and stack them in a corner with the cushions – perhaps the little ones would like to help you, and in the meantime perhaps your big brothers will wash the breakfast dishes and tidy the kitchen . . .'

The children gathered round her, and it was almost like being back at school. Provided that she spoke slowly and deliberately they understood her, the little girls dropping an awed curtsy and the boys touching their rough-cut forelocks when she impressed upon them that they were not to meddle with any of the kitchen equipment until they had learned how to use it properly. When she came to the end of her instructions the girl Dorcas murmured something inaudible and Eleanor had to ask her to repeat it.

'The girl asks for your blessing, mistress,' Jacob said.

Touched by the request Eleanor put out her hand to the bowed head. 'Bless you, Dorcas dear,' she said.

It was obvious that they had all seen the car standing out

60

in the lane on the previous evening, and when the baby had been fed and Eleanor had completed the shopping list the children accompanied them to the gate, watching with suppressed excitement as Eleanor opened the two rear doors and indicated to Jacob and Mary that they should get inside. They did so, not without a certain nervous reluctance on Mary's part, and before starting the engine Eleanor turned round to them from the driving seat.

'Now listen, both of you. This thing that we call a car will travel along the roads although you will not see anyone pulling it. The horses are inside it, in the form of many strange little cogs and wheels and things that even I do not understand. But you must remember that it is not worked by any kind of magic or supernatural power. It will not harm you. It is simply a modern mode of conveyance which everyone uses nowadays. Do you both understand?'

They nodded, waiting breathlessly. Eleanor started the engine, paused for a second or two and then engaged first gear. She began to edge forward, aware of Mary's suppressed gasp. They moved slowly past the gate, the children waving and one of them (she thought) crying, then they rounded the first bend in the lane and the cottage was lost to view.

She drove very slowly, easing the car over the ruts and bumps and keeping a close watch on her passengers through the driving mirror. They were sitting very close together, Mary staring blindly ahead while Jacob peered from one side to the other, bright with curiosity.

'Now don't forget,' Eleanor warned as they approached the hard road, 'that you will see lots of other cars of different shapes and sizes all going along by themselves. You must be prepared for things to be very different, but remember what I told you – nothing is going to harm you.'

They passed through several villages, and although most of them contained at least a sprinkling of old timbered buildings neither of the Dawes gave any sign of recognition. They might have been on Mars, and when they reached the main car park in the town she saw that there were beads of sweat on Jacob's forehead.

'Nothing – will – harm – you,' she repeated, turning

61

round and smiling at them before they got out of the car. 'People will be dressed differently, *everything* will be different, but it is all going to be *wonderful* and not *frightening*—'

They nodded speechlessly, and conscious that her own heart was beating fast she opened the car door and got out. They stood beside her, pale and flinching, and then with her handbag slung on her shoulder she took each of them by the arm and walked with them through the car park to the High Street. And the astonishing thing was that no one took the slightest notice of them.

Apart from the possibility that her two charges might bolt terror-stricken through the crowds, the one thing that Eleanor had feared had been the discomfort they would suffer if they were stared at. Yet no one gave them a glance. Mary in her long home-spun dress could have been any ordinary young woman wearing some kind of fashionable ethnic costume while Jacob in his rumpled breeches and belted blouse merely seemed to present one more variation on the theme of radical chic. If anyone had bothered to examine them against their new background of concrete and glass they would almost certainly have labelled them Arty and not Tudor.

So much for us, thought Eleanor, steering them into the supermarket. Trained only to observe what the media offers in the privacy of our homes our sense of curiosity is switched off whenever we go about the ordinary inescapable chores. When we go shopping we do just that, and nothing more. There is nothing extraneous worth looking at while we're waiting in the check-out queue; we know there isn't, because otherwise some conscientious and responsible expert would have presented it to us on the box.

In the whole of the town there was very probably only one person who might recognise Jacob and Mary Dawes for the living miracle they were; that person was Eric Seward, but for the present she had no intention of sharing them with anyone.

The shopping expedition was a complete success. They followed at her side, docile as two small pupils as she pushed the wire trolley past the shelves loaded with packets and tins, and they watched with reverence as she selected her purchases, often pausing to explain in a quiet easy voice what various commodities were for. About the only curious glance they provoked was from a woman who overheard Eleanor telling them that very few people bothered to mill their own flour these days.

After a while there was something almost playful about the way in which Jacob helped her to stack the simple basic foodstuffs into the trolley (Mary hung back with a timid smile), but the bleeping of the cashier's till seemed to cause them great uneasiness and Jacob jumped violently when the cash drawer in it suddenly shot open. Smiling sympathetically, Eleanor reached across to the plastic whirligig hung with confectionery and bought them both a bar of chocolate, and then had to explain in an undertone that it was something nice to eat.

'But you must remove the paper first,' she said, and thought: My children . . . they really are my *children* . . .

When the food had been transferred to the boot of the car she took them on impulse to Marks & Spencers, where Mary paused on the threshold.

'It is holy, like unto a church . . .'

Mindful of the tendency to fall on their knees, Eleanor took her arm and led her firmly into the store where the racks and stacks of identical clothes seemed to bewilder them even more than the supermarket.

'So who be all the people whose raiment hangs here?' Jacob asked in a hoarse whisper and Eleanor took them to a quiet place by the men's pants and vests and explained as briefly as possible the modern necessity for mass marketing. They nodded dumbly, then a little further on came to the women's clothes where Eleanor impulsively selected an ankle-length flowered cotton dress and held it up against Mary. She looked enquiringly across at Jacob, who grinned delightedly.

'Do you like it, Mary? Do you think it would suit you?'

Unable to speak, Mary nodded and passed trembling fingers down the front of it, then gave a little gasp of anguish when Eleanor removed it and took it over to the cash desk. She paid by cheque and then handed the dress back to Mary, who appeared as dazed by the plastic carrier bag as she was by the contents.

They bought Jacob some jeans and a sports shirt and it was impossible to resist the lure of the children's department. Excited out of her normal timidity Mary burrowed her hands deep into the piles of cotton shorts, frilly skirts and patterned tee-shirts, and to Eleanor who stood watching there was something wonderful and deeply moving about this wife and mother who had mysteriously stepped across the barrier of four hundred years, yet whose expression of absorbed appraisal was so precisely the same as those of her twentieth-century sisters engaged on the same task of choosing and selecting.

They bought and bought, and to Eleanor the cost no longer mattered. Only mazedly aware that she owed them a huge emotional debt of gratitude for building Jackdaw's Cottage and that she now loved them both as individuals, she wrote cheques and collected carrier bags and when the spree ended in Boots where she bought shaving equipment and finally a toothbrush for each one of them, Jacob burst into a sudden ear-splitting guffaw when she explained what they were for.

People stared, but his laughter became uncontrollable. Sagging at the knees, he held his ribs and made no attempt to stifle the huge roars of mirth, and it seemed incredible to the loving Eleanor that curious onlookers shouldn't recognise it for what it was; the marvellous, uninhibited laughter of England's Golden Age.

They drove home at normal speed, laughing, triumphant and happy, with Jacob sitting in front next to Eleanor while Mary rustled among the parcels in the back seat. They ate their chocolate, marvelling at the neat little square of it and lamenting bitterly when the silver paper tore. Shorn of their initial fear and confusion they now seemed able to surrender wholeheartedly to the wonders that crowded in on all sides, and seeing her own environment through their eyes made Eleanor freshly aware of its more obvious advantages. Once again it was hard to avoid a feeling of omnipotence, or to explain some of the simpler miracles of technology without inadvertently taking credit for them.

'That little shiny thing up there is called an aeroplane,' she said, pointing, 'and we invented them somewhere around the beginning of this century. We think nothing of travelling all round the world in them, and some of them go very fast indeed . . . faster than the speed of sound . . .'

It was still only eleven-thirty, for they had arrived at the supermarket shortly after nine, and the sky had now deepened to a hard glittering blue. Heat shimmered on the empty road and with a sigh of relief Eleanor turned down the lane where the trees met overhead.

'We can travel all over the world, but this is the very best place on earth,' she said. 'Down this old winding lane to the side of the valley and —' She hesitated, a little uncertain whether to say *my* cottage or *your* cottage, 'and the most beautiful little house that anyone could wish for.'

They seemed quite capable of understanding her sentiments and of accepting them with genuine pleasure, and when they passed the final bend in the rough track Eleanor slowed to a halt with a cry of delight. The children were coming to meet them, singing and skipping hand in hand through the twinkling sunlight. Seeing the car they broke into a run, the big ones helping the little ones along, and the wonderful laughing happiness of the reunion made it impossible to imagine that anything terrible could ever happen.

2

The Reverend Arthur Parsloe wandered down the centre aisle of his church, whisky glass in hand. Dust-laden sunlight fell across the box pews and highlighted here and there the malign gargoyle heads carved on the door jambs.

For a long while now he had taken only one service a month, and last Sunday had produced a congregation of three, one of whom was his wife. Until last Easter there had been four, but Mrs Agnew, aged eighty and dropsical, had at last taken to her bed and died. The funeral was tomorrow

65

at the crematorium.

'We did think about having it here,' her daughter had said with the air of someone prepared at least to consider any proposal, however outlandish, 'but to be quite honest, my husband and I don't think that burying people in the ground is healthy and I know I wouldn't like to think of Mum laying there among all them worms . . . the service is at 2.15 and of course you're more than welcome to come . . .'

Nice of her. Really most thoughtful. But if she imagined that he was going to play it her way she could think again. Have mercy upon us, O Lord, have mercy upon us for we are utterly despised. Our soul is filled with the scornful reproof of the wealthy and with the despitefulness of the proud . . . The silly fat cow could sling Mum in the river for all he cared.

Taking a large swig of whisky he held it in his mouth for a moment before tilting his head and allowing it to trickle slowly down his throat. It was a trick he had learned to do some while ago without choking.

But of course he did care. Poor old dame with her bloated limbs and her protruding pekinese eyes fixed on him as he ascended the pulpit. She seldom spoke to him – when she did it was only in a series of timid little country platitudes – yet during the Sunday morning sermon her eyes seemed to beseech him for some sort of help. She must have known that she was dying and one afternoon he called at her house because he wanted to talk to her and to hold her hand for a while. But he found that the doctor had arrived ten minutes before him. He sat in the stuffy little front room listening to the thump of feet and the murmur of voices overhead, and when it finally came to his turn the doctor poked his head round the door and said: 'I don't think I'd bother her just now – I've given her a shot of something and she's already feeling nice and drowsy . . . '

Unto thee I lift mine eyes, O thou that dwellest in the heavens.

Meandering on he came to the font, and lifting up the heavy oak cover saw mouse droppings in the bottom of it. He dropped the cover back in place with a dispirited thud and wandered back to the vestry. Refilling his glass he thought for some reason of the woman who had bought Jackdaw's Cottage. A nice-looking woman, but stupid. They all seemed to be stupid these days.

And there was nothing in this world more stupid than mooning over the past, whether it was a matter of centuries or days. It was the present which mattered – things like Cambodia, the plutonium bomb, animal laboratories, and one day he was going to shake off the lassitude that kept him tethered in this ridiculous rustic dump. He was going to break out, nail his true colours to the mast and join in the battle for positive practical good. He would tell the bishop that he intended to resign his living and he would give Bunty the opportunity to leave him or accompany him, whichever she preferred. He perched himself on the table, banging his feet together.

Yet there were occasions when even he couldn't help looking back to the past, slipping back into the skin of childhood with all its acute pleasures and pains and its warning messages for the adult who was to come.

The only son of missionary parents who had died of cholera, he had been brought up by his grandparents; loving gentle people who never said they hoped that one day he would train for the ministry without adding that he must always feel perfectly free to make his own choice. He could look back and see with great clarity the rambling house on Sydenham Hill and his grandmother in black silk and pince-nez reading Kipling's *Plain Tales from the Hills* to him while he was convalescing from a childish infection.

'God has seen fit to take two of our darlings from us,' she said when he asked if he might get dressed and go in the garden, 'and Grandpa and I believe that you have been spared in order to follow in His footsteps. So it would be rather selfish, wouldn't it Arthur dear, to go out and *deliberately* catch a fresh chill?'

Nervous and stumbling, with a big nose and a lot of big crooked teeth, he found at the age of eighteen that his decision whether or not to enter the church was expected daily, almost hourly. Very little was said, but the anxious, loving, querying glances were more than sufficient to fill him with pitiful agitation. On his knees in the privacy of his bedroom he begged God to give him a sign, but nothing happened. He thought of his parents' sacrifice and of the simple goodness of his grandparents and knew that he ought to be ordained. Perhaps they were right, and God had spared him from cholera for some special reason. Then he would think of the works of Bernard Shaw and of the Church's apparent indifference to Mussolini's invasion of Abyssinia, and know that he couldn't.

The problem was resolved quite simply in July 1937. The fox terrier pup called Sam whom his grandparents had given him for a birthday present developed what was then called distemper. Within hours he became transformed from a crisp springy thing of delight to a shivering, tormented bundle wrapped in a shawl in a darkened room. The vet came every morning, and on the third day Arthur walked out into the garden, looked up at the calm summer sky and said: 'Let him live and I'll follow in Your footsteps. If You let him die I'll go in the army.'

That evening Sam rallied. Dosed with bromide and strengthened with beef tea trickled into the side of his mouth, the terrible downhill slide seemed to have been arrested. They took it in turns to sit up with him, and on the morning that he lifted his head and feebly wagged his tail there was no longer any reason to prevaricate. In a gush of grateful, semi-hysterical tears Arthur told his grandparents that he wanted to take holy orders. Although he didn't mention it the reservations were still there, but having witnessed Sam's recovery he was now prepared to believe that he would receive divine help in dealing with them. In any case he had given his word.

His grandparents also wept, but in their case it was with unadulterated joy and he went up to Cambridge that Michaelmas with two new suits and an allowance which he knew was more than they could really afford. Two weeks after his arrival he received a letter to say that poor dear little Sam had slipped his collar in frenzied pursuit of a cat and had been run over by the laundry van.

'It's all so bloody stupid,' the Reverend Parsloe said to the empty air. 'Examination of the past brings nothing but pain and a desire for oblivion . . .'

He drained his glass, replaced it behind the parish registers in the cupboard and told himself that very soon now he was going to take off. He was getting out, packing it in, quitting the scene, and so far as he was concerned, God, that cynical purveyor of worthless promises, could take unto Himself a running jump.

He fumbled in his pocket for the tube of peppermints.

Over at Jackdaw's Cottage the presents had been distributed, the foodstuffs put away, and after a snack lunch they were all in the sitting-room. Mary in her new cotton dress was nursing the baby, the smaller children were crouched on the floor absorbed in a pile of interlocking toy bricks and Eleanor watched young Dorcas stepping carefully round them as she collected the wrapping paper and carrier bags and folded them reverently.

While the abrupt change into twentieth-century dress had obviously altered their appearance considerably, to Eleanor there still remained a strange, other-world quality about them; the scent of herbs and old churches persisted, and the little girls in their dirndl skirts and Mickey Mouse tee-shirts still bobbed a curtsy when spoken to. But there was something else; something mysterious and intangible that lay beneath the warm flesh and blood, and she could only compare it to the muted glamour that seems to cling for an hour or two to people who have just arrived from a faraway country. Their skins still bear the scent of foreign soap and exotic cooking, just as their eyes are still full of other sights, other scenes. But in the case of Jacob Dawes and his family the miracle was that they were still bathed in the sunlit harmony of Gloriana and Will Shakespeare. The thought filled her with a profound delight.

One of the two older boys came towards her, wearing a tartan shirt over his old homespun breeches. She remembered that his name was Ned, and it struck her that he was walking strangely. Then she began to laugh.

'Oh look, Ned, you've got your shoes on the wrong feet!'

The boy halted, and stood scrutinising his new canvas sneakers.

'Not so.'

'Yes, you have. Look, if you put your feet together the toes point sideways. Can't you see?'

He looked at the shoes again, and then at her. 'Not so.'

Suddenly aware that the room had fallen silent Eleanor raised her eyes and saw Jacob standing in the doorway.

The jeans he was wearing fitted low on the hips and his own heavy leather belt was threaded through the loops. The flowered shirt they had chosen for him accentuated his strong neck and the thick brown bob of hair which he had obviously brushed, yet looking across at him she would have said that he looked by far the least contemporary of the family. The impression he gave was somehow that of a peasant who had assumed the clothing suitable to a gentleman of his own era. A country squire accustomed to fine linen, she thought, but not the doublet and hose, slashed velvet and brocade of a courtier. Intercepting her glance he doffed an imaginary cap and swept a low bow, evidently aware of his family's open-mouthed admiration.

'Very nice, Jacob,' Eleanor said lightly. 'I was just telling your son that he's wearing his new shoes on the wrong feet.'

Jacob walked across to where the boy stood, glanced down and then said: 'Change them.'

'They give no offence,' Ned muttered.

'Change them.'

'Why so?'

'Because mistress orders,' Jacob said, and abruptly dealt him a ringing blow on the ear. Ned staggered and fell against the low telephone table. The bowl of roses on it skidded and hit the wall in a splash of water. The bowl broke.

Eleanor started towards it with a cry of dismay, then paused. The boy Ned was sitting on the floor, holding his ear and rocking to and fro.

'Jacob, you should never hit a child on the ear like that. It could cause permanent damage.'

'A child should not disobey its father,' Jacob replied, then turned to Dorcas. 'Attend to the disorder.'

Laying aside the pile of wrapping paper she hastened across the room and began to separate the spilled roses

70

from the broken china. Wet petals clung to her hands. The other children continued to stare in silence as Ned held his ear and emitted a snuffling whimpering sound.

'Get you gone before I clout the other,' Jacob said, shoving at him. Scrambling hastily to his feet Ned stumbled out into the garden.

Without speaking Eleanor went over to help Dorcas. She mopped the table dry with a cloth from the kitchen, then in order to cause a diversion pointed to the telephone and asked her if she knew what it was. Dorcas shook her head.

'It's called a tel-e-phone. It was invented – *made*, if you like – by a man called Alexander Graham Bell sometime around the 1870s. It was a very clever invention because it enables us to talk to one another when we're a long distance apart.'

Dorcas stood meekly to attention with her eyes cast down.

'Would you like to try it? You can even dial someone to tell you the time – the Speaking Clock, it's called – you just put your finger in the numbers 8-0-8-1 and then if you hold this part of it to your ear you'll hear the voice . . .'

The girl flinched at the sharp *ting* as Eleanor removed the receiver from its rest. She watched the demonstration in silence.

'D'you see? Good. Now you do it. Finger in 8, then 0 . . . Ah, haven't you learned to count, Dorcas? Don't you know the alphabet? Well, never mind. Look, like this . . .'

Taking the girl's hand in her own Eleanor guided her finger, and was unprepared for the expression of horror which slowly dawned in her eyes at the sound of the disembodied voice. With a little gasp she thrust the receiver back at Eleanor, who replaced it and then swiftly took the girl's arm.

'Nothing is going to harm you, Dorcas. Nothing whatever. All of you are perfectly safe here with me. Do you understand that?'

Very reluctantly the girl raised her large blue-grey eyes and whispered that she did. Then managed a little faltering, trembling smile in which Eleanor thought she detected the

71

first real hint of amity.

But it can't be rushed, she thought. We've got to take it very slowly . . .

On the other side of the room Mary picked up the closely swaddled baby – so far Eleanor had caught no more than a glimpse of it – and prepared to take it upstairs. She too seemed to be getting used to the place, moving unobtrusively about her small quiet tasks and acknowledging Eleanor's presence with a polite bob of the head. One of these days I'll be able to have a real conversation with her, Eleanor thought. She watched her carry the baby upstairs, and then became aware that Jacob was no longer in the room. The small children had returned to their play and she wandered out into the garden, vaguely intending to find Ned and to enquire about his ear.

The heat seemed intense after the cool of the sitting-room. Rising like a solid force from the old paving stones it licked at her face, sticking her hair flat against her forehead and moistening her upper lip. Shielding her eyes with her hand she walked slowly past the comfortable mounds of lavender and box and the spires of madonna lilies. The earth, where she could see it, looked pale and exhausted and she told herself that with the cool of evening nothing would be simpler than to organise the children into a watering party; a length of garden hose attached to the stand pipe would be a novelty, but not, she thought, a frightening one. In fact it had all the potential of a happy pre-bedtime romp and she smiled as she pictured the smaller girls leaping and squealing as they dodged the glittering spray. Perhaps Mary might even allow them to take off their clothes . . .

She turned into the back garden, following the narrow twisting path that ran between the old fruit trees and the roses, and although there was no sign of Ned she came quite suddenly upon Jacob. He was standing by the low boundary hedge, twisting a sprig of it in his fingers and staring across the little valley, and he appeared so absorbed and intent that she hesitated for a moment before making her presence known.

'Has it changed much, Jacob?'

He nodded, without altering the direction of his gaze.

'I'm sorry.' It seemed a stupid thing to say, but she couldn't help it.

'Later men than I have put away the little doddy bit fields. Can't see Sheepfold or Hobb's Pasture or Nine Corners . . . used to be a fine clump of oaks over there, see.'

She went closer, staring in the direction of his pointing finger. There were no oaks there now; only a smooth sea of blue-green corn.

'On a fair day you could view across to Polford Mill. Ought to see it now, but for the summer haze laying its hand on the distance. Ole Miller Speedwell's a rare ole boy with a barrel of ale. He'll sink half a firkin between sunrest and first light and then be about his work merry as a lark. His eldest gal married my half-brother and they dwell over Grafton way—'

'Live?'

He turned to face her, and it seemed as if he were subjecting her to the same intent scrutiny that he had given to the valley.

'I don't feel as if I'm dead, mistress.'

Had there been any lingering doubt about the reality of the situation it would have been finally dispelled by the proximity of the man and by the challenge in his eyes. She saw for the first time that they were red-brown in colour – fox colour, she thought involuntarily. She also saw that there was a pock-mark on his forehead, a faint circular indentation between the left eyebrow and the thick fringe of his hair. Standing there in the dazzling sunlight he seemed now to be more intensely alive than other ordinary people. People like Eric Seward, for instance.

'Don't disturb my peace, Jacob,' she said quietly.

'You brought us back.'

'I didn't. How could I?'

'I've not the wit to explain. But if you can make a wheeled thing go along the turnpike without horse or oxen to draw it, if you can make daylight come at your bidding and water to run and all the elements obey you, then it was child's work for you to bring us here. All you did was to pray into the – the' – he made a small circular movement with his index finger – 'and you made it to happen.'

'No one's yet found a way to talk to God on the telephone, so far as I know,' she said wryly.

He turned his attention to the valley again, then said abruptly: 'Where is your husband?'

'He's dead.'

'Did you love and honour him?'

'Yes. I did.'

He turned to her fiercely. 'Then why in the name of God did you not recall *him* to the living world?'

'But I tell you I didn't —' Her voice rose.

'But what's to be the end of it?'

'I don't know.'

They remained silent for a moment, both staring across the corn and feeling the sun's heat on their shoulders. To Eleanor it felt as if it were trying to press her into the ground, to demolish her. It was an effort to speak calmly.

'I don't know what the end is going to be, Jacob, but we mustn't be frightened of each other, or of what's happened. It's not the need for an explanation that's important, it's the fact that now we're faced with each other we've got to be very careful not to upset the balance. This frail sort of relationship we've begun to establish —' She broke off, aware of his incomprehension. 'Sorry, Jacob, more stupid modern words, when all I'm really trying to say is – well, trust me.'

She held out her hand, and after a moment's hesitation he took it.

'Trust me, Jacob, and I'll trust you. After all, I suppose we've no alternative.'

'Trust?'

'Yes.' She felt the rough dry strength of his hand. 'I trust you not to – to harm me.'

'I'd be a fool to harm you, mistress,' he said slowly. 'You with all your powerful ways.'

'That's not what I mean. You're talking about trust based on fear. Let it be a trust built on mutual esteem – we all like each other as *friends*. You see, once I'd got over the shock of your appearing last night I could only see it as

74

some kind of wonderful miracle. I was very happy and excited because living in your house like this had made me think about you a lot. And working on the assumption – I mean, believing that one day you'll all disappear just as suddenly as you appeared, we must teach each other and – and *enjoy* each other as much as we can, mustn't we?'

Continuing to hold her hand he stood watching her steadily, and the strange, rather challenging silence between them was suddenly ripped by the sound of a woman's terrified scream coming from the cottage.

They turned sharply and began to run towards it, united by the immediate realisation that if people could return from the dead there was no longer any limit to what was possible, for either good or evil.

3

But after the initial shock the evil which awaited them was not irreparable, for Eleanor at any rate.

The kitchen was in turmoil. At first it was difficult to ascertain the true situation because the place seemed to be full of weeping and demented children scurrying to and fro and it was instinct alone which made her clap her hands together and call loudly and authoritatively for silence. And as in the old days at school, she was instinctively obeyed.

Three rings on the electric hob were glaring red, one of them nibbling at a tea towel which lay flung down close to it, and the sink was brimming with water which trickled in a small river down the front of the unit and on to the tiled floor. Dense steam from the kettle had all but obliterated the ceiling and there was blood pouring from a cut on one of the little girls' fingers. Mary, with her hair tied up in a cloth, was sobbing and running like the sorcerer's apprentice from one catastrophe to another.

'*Stop* – all of you!' Eleanor clapped her hands again, then moved swiftly between the motionless, frightened figures, turning off the cooker rings, and dousing the smouldering tea towel in the sink before letting out the water. She produced a tin of Band-Aid from the cupboard, cleaned the child's cut and covered it with a dressing. She mopped the floor with the remains of the wrung-out tea towel then reached down a brightly coloured tin and gave all the children a biscuit before telling them to go and play in the garden. Bobbing little curtsies and hastily touching their forelocks they did so.

'And now,' she said, turning to Jacob who was standing with his arm round his wife, 'I think we could all do with a drink. Could you pour us a sherry each, please, Jacob? The pale brown stuff in the decanter on the tray with the glasses.'

He went through to the sitting-room while Mary stood wiping her eyes on the hem of her long dress.

'Don't cry, Mary dear.' Eleanor went over to her. 'It was very thoughtless of me to leave you here with all this—'

''Tis magic . . .'

'No, not magic – technology.' She touched Mary lightly on the shoulder. 'We don't believe in the powers of magic any more. We only believe in the things we can understand. And although I personally can't claim to understand exactly how all this works' – she indicated the kitchen equipment with a wave of the hand – 'lots of other people can – they're called electrical engineers – and they can make things or mend them when they go wrong so that ordinary people like me – yes, and like you too, Mary – can use them and benefit from them. Do you understand?'

She spoke with a slow, quiet emphasis, holding Mary's fluttering and unwilling gaze with her own. 'Do you understand, Mary dear, that there is no such thing as magic? There is only tech-no-logy – which is rather a difficult word for you to remember, isn't it?'

Jacob returned with the tray. Setting it down he carefully filled each sherry glass to the brim and they sat down at the kitchen table, smiling at one another and sighing with relief.

'It's not at all easy for you to grasp all the changes which have taken place in the world during the past four hundred

76

years,' Eleanor continued benevolently, 'but I promise that I will do everything I can to help you.'

Jacob nodded, then downed his sherry at a gulp. He refilled his glass. 'This is a merry tipple.'

'Yes, taken in small quantities.' Unobtrusively Eleanor replaced the stopper in the decanter. 'And now we've had time to recover our breath we ought to be thinking about preparing supper – I'm sure the children must be getting hungry. Mary, perhaps you could help to peel some potatoes while I see to some of the other things . . .'

Sipping her sherry she planned the meal. It would be wise to keep it simple, and with eight mouths to feed (not counting the baby) she decided to defrost two steak and mushroom pies and to concoct a pudding from ice cream, which would make an interesting novelty for her guests. After supplying Mary with the potatoes and a sharp knife she went through to the dining-room to set the table.

It was cooler in there, and the chanting of children's voices floated pleasantly through an open window. It was suddenly rather agreeable to be on her own and she leaned her forehead against the window frame, thinking disconnectedly about the past twenty-four hours. This time yesterday she had been prepared for nothing more startling than a visit from the man from the Record Office (what was his name? Ah yes, Eric Seward), and now the place was humming with the presence of a man and his wife and six children. Even on the rare occasions when there was no one in sight the atmosphere in and around the cottage seemed to be full of them, and already the whistling of stiff new jeans had become blended in her mind with the haunting fugitive scent of herbs and old damp stone.

A soft footfall made her turn round. Jacob was examining the dinner service displayed on the open shelves of the big oak dresser.

'Gentlemen's platters . . .'

'Plates,' she corrected automatically, and moved towards the drawer for the knives and forks.

'We call them platters.'

She paused beside him, smiling. 'Look – whose age are we living in?'

His red-brown eyes smiled back at her, but she became aware of their challenge. Without speaking they continued to stare at one another, and it seemed as if she had won a minor victory when he looked away first.

'Platters or plates,' he said with a shrug, 'the only concern is that they are filled with good meat.'

Graciously she agreed, and after counting out the cutlery began to set it down either side of the table, placing herself at the head of it.

Supper was ready by seven o'clock and the children were puzzled but compliant when she instructed them to wash their hands and faces before sitting down to eat.

Mary and Dorcas helped her to carry in the dishes and when everyone was seated she began to cut and portion out the steak and mushroom pies while a buzz of eager conversation rose on both sides. And then it ceased abruptly. Having served herself last of all she looked up sharply and saw that every head was bowed over clasped hands and that all eyes were tightly closed. They looked rapt and touchingly devout, and once more she became aware of the immense gulf which separated her from them. Love filled her, and although she quietly replaced her knife and fork by her plate and put her hands together in the attitude of prayer she couldn't bring herself to close her eyes.

'Praise the Lord, ye servants; O praise the name of the Lord,' intoned Jacob. 'Blessed be the name of the Lord from this time forth for evermore. Amen.'

Amen,' his family repeated.

Then the buzz of conversation started again and Eleanor's voice rose above it as she called to one of the two bigger boys: 'We generally use a tablespoon to help ourselves to vegetables; look, there's one by the dish . . .'

But it was too late. They all helped themselves with their fingers, scooping up the peas and the new buttery potatoes with quick, neat movements and then using their pudding spoons instead of knives and forks. She decided not to comment, suspecting that they would soon notice her own correct way of eating and copy it.

They all seemed very hungry, and Eleanor saw Jacob assisting one of the smaller girls, breaking up the squares of

78

glistening steak with his fingers and then wiping them down the front of his new shirt. She looked away, and in doing so found herself watching Mary push peas on to her spoon with her finger. Their eyes met, and although Eleanor smiled encouragement Mary laid aside her spoon as if her appetite had suddenly fled. It now occurred to Eleanor that her own table manners must appear strange and finicking by comparison. She put down her knife and ate with her fork, but that, she thought, merely made her look like an American. (Still, they wouldn't know that. She doubted whether they'd even heard of the place.)

Although Jacob appeared pleasantly at ease she became aware that the atmosphere was growing strained, the buzz of conversation gradually diminishing to an occasional furtive whisper, and in an effort to restore the mood to its former cheerfulness Eleanor asked Mary if she liked cooking.

'Yes, mistress.' The reply was barely audible.

'You're not eating much. Come along now . . .'

Mary shook her head, and familiar now with her habit of timid withdrawal Eleanor decided to ignore her.

'You grow a strange little turnip, mistress,' Jacob said with his mouth full. 'But they have a comely taste.' He helped himself to more.

'You know I didn't grow them, Jacob, because you saw me buy them. And they're potatoes, not turnips.'

He continued to eat, busily and good-humouredly. 'Do you always buy everything, mistress? Meats and breads and eggs? You lack for nothing, yet you turn your hand to nothing yourself. Is this how your world is ordered?'

'I'm afraid it is, these days. It's what we call a consumer society, and as far as food is concerned, it's no longer an economic proposition to grow small amounts here and there. Everything is done in bulk—'

'Did you buy your husband, mistress? Did you see him for sale among a score of others in the big market? Sitting on a shelf, waiting to be taken down and wheeled away like a sack of corn?'

Eleanor refused to be needled. She spoke slowly and very gently. 'Oh, no. I'm glad to say that we still meet people and fall in love with one another in the same way that people have always done.'

The two big boys at the far end of the table sniggered audibly and Dorcas glanced at them from under her lashes. Determined to ignore them, Eleanor leaned her elbows on the table and stared hard at Jacob.

'Please tell me what it was like for you, living here. It's strange, you know, but I've always wanted to travel in time the way other people travel to different places. It's never enough just to *read* about what happened – I want to have been there and seen it for myself. I'd give anything to have been at Tilbury, for instance, when your Queen made her speech to the troops: "My loving people, we have been persuaded by some that are careful of our safety to take heed how we commit ourselves to armed multitudes for fear of treachery; but I reassure you, I do not desire to live in distrust of my faithful and loving people . . ." I loved that speech so much when I was at school that I learned it off by heart. And I think that of all the characters in history I would rather have met Elizabeth Tudor than any other. Have you ever caught sight of her on one of her progresses through this part of the country? Or do you know of anyone who has?'

Looking down the table she saw that they were all regarding her with an expression of total incomprehension. Chilled, she tried to laugh it off.

'The trouble is that I've got the broad framework of history while you've got all the teeming irrelevancies of one little patch, and there seems to be hardly any relationship between the two. In some ways I'd probably come closer to your century with a modern professor of history than I do with you. Yet all of you are the essence – the marvellous reality of that time, and I want you to share it with me in the same way that I'm sharing my modern outlook and experience with you.'

'What year is this, mistress, by your reckoning?' asked Jacob, licking his fingers.

'It's an established fact that it's 1981. The twenty-fourth of July, to be precise.' She switched her attention to the eldest girl. 'And I'll tell you something very interesting,

Dorcas. Do you know that we have a Queen Elizabeth as well? Queen Elizabeth the Second. And sometimes there are fears for her safety too, when she goes among her subjects, which shows you that in some ways things haven't changed all that much, have they?'

The girl sat with her eyes downcast. Listening, but too shy to answer. During the little silence which followed, someone belched loudly.

'So don't you want to know about some of the things that have happened in the world since you lived here, Jacob?' Eleanor persisted.

'The world's a big place, mistress.'

'Well, things that have happened in this country, then. For example, would it shock you to know that in 1649 we English people executed our King and instituted a Commonwealth?'

He looked up at her cheerfully, his mouth full. 'So be it, mistress.' Then he darkened, his eyebrows drawing together beneath the thick fringe of bobbed hair. 'But what became of Polford Mill? The haze has cleared and it should be in view, but there's naught to see but corn and such.'

'I don't know,' she admitted. 'I suppose there are bound to have been changes of that sort, as well. But if you like, we'll try and find out . . . '

She sat back in her chair, idly watching as one of the older boys left the table and made for the nearest corner. He stood there with his back to the room and it was a second or two before she associated his stance with the sudden sharp splashing sound.

She leaped, her face pink with shocked anger. 'William – for God's sake! I showed all of you how the lavatory works – there's one downstairs and one upstairs – you *can't* have forgotten!'

She looked to his parents for their reaction, and then at the rest of the family, but no one said anything. Those who were eating continued to do so. The boy returned to the table and she saw Jacob give his head a good-natured cuff before heaping his plate with more food. With a set face she pushed back her chair and walked out of the room.

She went into the garden. The air had cooled now and

the sky was covered with a thin high cloud. Across the lane from the cottage a blackbird was singing a muted sub-song as if getting in tune for the evening's performance and she leaned her arms on the gate, listening to it and feeling the anger slowly slip away. It was stupid to become upset because of a moment's forgetfulness, a careless return to a habit which must have been taken for granted by all and sundry in 1580. A bowlful of hot water with plenty of disinfectant would soon put William's misdemeanour right, and she told herself that she must sternly resist any tendency towards turning into a house-proud old maid. For some reason she had been given a chance in a million to play hostess to a family of people restored and revitalised from the Tudor dynasty, and it was only natural that a few upsets and misunderstandings would occur in the process.

She turned round from the gate and looked back at the cottage with loving eyes. The old peg tiles on the roof still seemed to glow with the warmth of the day's sun and she realised that the blackbird's song had given place to the hum of human voices coming from the open dining-room window; the voices of the people who had lived there when the house was young. The house belonged to them, she was a mere interloper, and as she listened to the sound floating out into the calm evening it was impossible to remain unaware of the fact that their animation had doubled since her departure from the room. She even heard Mary laughing.

She was still standing by the gate when the two little girls ran out of the front door. They appeared to be somewhere between the ages of five and seven, and it was an oversight on her part that she hadn't yet learned their names. Familiar and yet still strangely alien, they ran hand in hand down the path and their bubbling laughter was so infectious that her own lips twitched in sympathy. They ran past her, out into the lane and away through the trees as if they knew every stick and stone of the place, and their swift childish glee excluded her entirely. She had never felt more extraneous, and instinct suddenly told her that no matter how hard she tried, this was how it was bound to be.

Slowly she went indoors to find the ice cream.

4

Night came as no more than a thickening of the dark grey and purple shadows, and lying in bed the Reverend Arthur Parsloe waited with closed eyes for the small jerky movements that epitomised his wife's final preparations for sleep. The first jerk was caused by the brisk tug to the hem of her nightgown so that it fitted neatly about her ankles, and jerks two and three described the downward tug of each long full sleeve so that she shouldn't wake in the chill of early dawn with bare forearms. Already her broad back was warm against his and he waited for the final ritualistic words that never failed; words which for a long time now had afforded him a sad and hollow amusement. *Good night, darling boy, may God bless you and keep you.*

Bless me, heavenly Father, for I have transgressed. Although come to think of it, why should You be asked to bless a degenerate, and a moral swindler? For that's what I am, a swindler, a Laodicean, a disparager and a drunk . . . It's a sheer waste of time, O Lord – if You're there, that is . . .

But instead of blessing him she gave a final contented twitch to her nightgown and said: 'I can't help thinking that we ought to do something about that nice Mrs Millard.'

'Mrs Millard?' His nose was half-buried in the pillow.

'Over at Jackdaw's Cottage.'

'Uh-huh.'

'She said she'd been a school-teacher and it's ridiculous that she should shut herself away. She could give a hand with the Little Owls and Kingfishers now that Miss Glossop's retired.'

'She's a mourning widow.'

'Rubbish. She's merely in need of a little encouragement.'

83

The Reverend Parsloe floated in sleep. Little gold dots rose and fell behind his closed eyes and he seemed to hear the soft surging of a huge and patient ocean. Perhaps the little dots were birds . . .

'Did you find out anything about her cottage?'

'No.' He tried to think of a gold-coloured bird, but couldn't. The nearest he could get to it was the great skua, but even that was more brown than gold. Most sea birds were either white or pale grey.

'People need encouragement, Arthur.'

'Yes, I know.'

Floating. Little gold dots like scraps of confetti flung against a summer sky. In 1965 he had pinned a notice in the church porch forbidding the throwing of confetti in the vicinity unless the throwers were prepared to sweep it all up again afterwards. The notice had faded, become yellow and curled, and during a fierce March gale had burst from its drawing pin and blown away. There had not been any confetti for many years now. Neither had there been any weddings. Soon, there would be no divine worship of any sort.

'I think I may call on her tomorrow. I've got to see Mr Dainton about the parish mag and if I come back through Polford End I could nip across to her place and see how she's getting on. She'd probably be very glad to see a friendly face . . .'

Nose in pillow. Floating, with arms folded and soles of feet pressed against those of his wife. Misery, guilt and despair dissolving in the beautiful calm sea of sleep.

'She could also help with the adult literacy classes in September. Yes, I'll definitely call on her tomorrow. Good night, darling boy, may God bless you and keep you . . . .'

During the course of the afternoon Eric Seward had written another brief note, this time on office paper, to Eleanor Millard to thank her for a pleasant evening and once more to wish her well in Jackdaw's Cottage. Was she, as a matter of interest, proposing to take any steps to alter the name from Jackdaw's to Jacob Dawes'? He gathered that it only entailed giving written notice to the Post Office . . . He

84

stamped the envelope and handed it to the junior for posting.

For some reason Mrs Millard had been in his thoughts all day, and lying in bed that night he watched the reflection of car headlights on the ceiling and wished that he could see her again. He wasn't attracted to her in a physical sense but she possessed a particular sort of quality of which he seemed curiously in need. Serenity? Yes, she had that. Plus a quiet and agreeable maturity that was very inviting. Inviting, but not really in a physical sense.

A car stopped outside and he supposed that it was Corinne back from whatever pub or party she had gone to. But it drove on again almost immediately and there was no sound of footsteps along the path; no scuffling or giggling, or fumbling with the latch key. In any case it was not yet midnight. Corinne never came home before three or four in the morning; sometimes when she was feuding with him she didn't come home at all.

He had given up trying to help her through the black moods of rage and self-pity that swamped her, sometimes for weeks. He had discovered no way of reaching her through either love or reason, and sympathy seemed to exacerbate her more than anything. He had tried with diligence to follow the wild ramifications of her mind, to find a pathway through the maze of suspicions and torments but always he had to retreat, baffled and aghast that an intelligent being could get it all so wrong. He had tried to talk it over with her mother, hinting that she might need psychiatric treatment even as he himself probed, rather clumsily, for some childhood clue to her behaviour. But his mother-in-law, a large listless woman, merely remarked that Corinne wasn't mad she was wicked, and refused to discuss the matter any further.

Divorce had been considered several times, but despite the see-sawing of her emotions Corinne remained adamant in her refusal to settle for less than she had now. He would have to leave her with the house, the car, the children, and how he would afford to set up a separate home for himself was his problem. So they lived together separately; sometimes she was there and sometimes she wasn't. Every now and then she would tidy herself up, stop smelling of marijuana and cook regular meals. She was a very good cook, and after she had put the children to bed (laughter, splashing and the singing of nursery rhymes), she would sit with a pile of mending on her lap and talk about their funny sayings and their little ailments with a loving pride utterly at variance with the periods of indifference and neglect. He was certain now that she was schizophrenic, and commonsense told him that he should seize an opportunity during one of her rational spasms to persuade her to seek some sort of medical help, but his courage always failed him. There was so little happiness in their lives that it was monstrous to think of deliberately plunging them back into a misery of recrimination and deliberate misunderstanding before her change of mood should render it inevitable.

Linking his hands behind his head he returned to thinking of pleasanter things in general, and of Mrs Millard in particular. He wondered what she was doing at that moment (ten minutes to twelve), and whether she was in bed or not. If she was still up he envisaged her sitting in a chair in that beautiful honey-coloured room with her feet tucked under her while she read a book. Jane Austen or perhaps George Eliot, if she wasn't deep in a study of sixteenth-century English social history, for she loved the cottage, he told himself, with the mind of a scholar and the heart of a romantic. But if, like him, she was in bed (and he pictured her in a beautiful uncrumpled nightgown with little bows on the shoulders), she was probably lying there staring at the ceiling with her hands behind her head, thinking of her husband. He had noticed the photograph of a man on her bedside table when she showed him over the cottage, and had assumed that it was he. She was probably lying there longing for him – *I had so much happiness,* he remembered her saying – and he wished that he could comfort her in some way.

The door opened and a small white figure stood hesitantly in the shaft of light from the landing.

'Daddy, Pauly's been sick in my bed.'

'Oh, God. Badly?' He sat up.

'Yes. Baked beans and stuff.'

'Well, what was he doing in your bed?'

'He was lonely,' the child said. 'And I was, too.'

'Okay,' said her father, plodding barefoot towards her. 'Go down to the kitchen for a bucket while I—'

'Daddy . . .'

'What?'

'I think it's a bug.'

'Why?'

'I'm going to be sick too . . .'

Once again the night seemed unwilling to darken beyond a deep pearly-grey, and Eleanor lay staring at her open bedroom window and thinking for the first time since Sunday evening about Mo. She remembered her rather weird awareness of another presence in the vicinity, and her loving assumption that it was his. She wished that he was with her now, so that he could be sharing her amazed gratification at the family's return, and, in a minor degree, that he might confirm their reality and her sanity. (For although she had no doubt of either, additional reassurance on both scores would still be rather pleasant.)

She turned towards his photograph, staring at the outline of the frame and seeing in her mind's eye the strong body and the laughing, boisterous face above the garland of clinging seaweed. He would have handled the Dawes family so well; she remembered his light easy touch with difficult pupils, his ability to make and maintain a friendship in which authority apparently had no part, and she wondered, not for the first time, just how much of it had been a happy gift of nature and how much a carefully cultivated skill. Whichever it was, she wished she could be more like him.

I mustn't become a houseproud old maid, she thought. I mustn't mind when things get soiled or broken, and I must learn to see myself through their eyes. I must be able to laugh at the modern behavioural fashions and habits they find so preposterous. I must give them affection – which I already do, my God I do – but I must also try to give them some of Mo's geniality, his *inspiration* . . .

Tired by the day's events she drifted to the edge of slumber, and Mo seemed to go with her. The cottage was deathly quiet; no sounds of breathing or sighing or of bodies shifting in sleep. No creak of floorboards or sudden sharp crack of an old timber contracting in the cool after the day's heat. Sometimes the fridge down in the kitchen made a soft humming sound, but not tonight. And out in the garden the roses hung motionless, like little pale clusters of ghosts.

A dawn mist was rising when she was jerked abruptly awake. She sat up, gasping and blinking confusedly. Nothing moved, and there was no sound. She remained motionless, listening and waiting for her heart to stop its pounding. She realised that she had been dreaming, and strove to remember what about. The Dawes, she thought; something to do with the Dawes family, but the details remained elusive. She got out of bed and crept across to the window. Shreds of mist lay over the garden, hiding the smaller flowers and caressing the tall ones with its ethereal chiffon, and watching the first pink flush of sunrise the dream began to come back to her.

She had dreamed that the Dawes family was dying. All of them, even the baby, lying outstretched in a row on damp foetid straw with their hands clasped on their breasts and their eyes, wide and terrible, fixed on some distant and immovable point. She had bent over them, staring into their glistening faces and urging them back to life. She would help them, look after them, share everything she had with them if only they would make the effort to go on living. But when in her urgency she seized Jacob's arm it crumbled in her hand, dry and dust, and as she watched, horrified, the dust particles reassembled in the form of a million little pale insects that leaped and scuttered to safety in the straw.

She remained by the window, grateful for the cool air on her face while she told herself that it was a good thing she had remembered the dream. Now she wouldn't be tormented by hints and half-recollections of it; defused thus of its fearfulness, it could sink and fade to nothingness while she occupied her mind with practicalities.

But it made her wonder for the first time what the Dawes

had died of. And then, with a sharp intake of the breath, she realised that they must all have died at the ages they were now. Jacob and Mary, somewhere about her own age, and the children – the poor children . . . Most probably it would have been some sort of epidemic.

She couldn't ask them, because presumably they wouldn't know, but the idea led her to wonder if *they* wondered; if even now Jacob and Mary were lying awake and tormented by the effort of trying to remember why and how they had died, and whether any alternative action on their part could have averted the death of all their children.

I must try and talk to them, she thought. For although we believe their generation to have accepted death far more philosophically than we do, I must try to find out whether any such thoughts are worrying them; if not, I must be careful not to arouse them. But supposing they had all died of the plague, for instance? And supposing, oh my God supposing they had brought it back with them? She had read somewhere that the disease was transmitted by the bite from the species of flea associated with the black rat, and in the strengthening light she peered down at the two small bumps on her forearm which she had automatically assumed were mosquito bites. But just supposing they weren't.

She must find out. But how? Go to a doctor and say, Excuse me, but I've reason to believe I've been in contact with bubonic plague? She grimaced. Of course, old parish records would most probably contain a note of any outbreaks in the district at about the time of the Dawes; then she remembered the vicar's grudging and perfunctory announcement that the parish registers contained no entries earlier than 1640. There was no help to be had from that direction.

Panic mounted, filling her with a terrified sense of isolation. Suddenly she wanted them all to go. To leave the cottage in the same way in which they had arrived because she hadn't the strength or the wisdom to deal with them. Loving concern for them was not sufficient protection from all the strange and chilling consequences which could result from the situation. They must go, they must go—

The frightened patter of her thoughts was arrested by a tap on the door. She stood rigid, willing herself to be calm. Then drawing a deep shuddering breath she went across and opened it.

Mary stood there, holding a small basin in both hands. She was wearing some kind of coarse cotton shift which Eleanor subconsciously registered as having been a petticoat to her original dress. Her hair hung down her back in a rough plait and her face looked pinched and apprehensive.

'I bid you good morning, mistress,' she whispered, proffering the basin.

Eleanor took it, a little uncertainly, as Mary bobbed a curtsy and hastily retreated.

Back in her room Eleanor closed the door before examining the contents. A plain white basin from the kitchen, it was full of cold milk with small chunks of bread floating in it. There was no spoon.

She remained staring at it, and the idea that Mary had voluntarily brought her what must presumably be the Tudor version of breakfast in bed moved her deeply. Her fears evaporated and she began to laugh silently, holding the bowl close against her while over in the valley the first larks rose up singing merrily from the corn.

5

And the weather, on that final day, promised perfection. The sun's rays, turning from pink to gold, touched the last pale shreds of mist and dispersed them. The sky turned to a delicate blue behind the haze and the garden sparkled beneath an unusually heavy dew. It was the kind of morning which seems to touch everything with its own radiant beauty, and to promise every living creature a taste of incomparable joy during the hours to come.

The family breakfasted in the kitchen, intrigued by the bright packets of rustling cereal that Eleanor had bought in the supermarket. She sat with them, drinking coffee and saying again how much she had appreciated her bowl of bread and milk. The atmosphere was one of cordial and well-mannered restraint, and studying them unobtrusively she could read no sign of undue stress in the faces of either Jacob or Mary. She realised now that it would probably never occur to them to waste time wondering what they had died of; life as they had known it would have been too hard and too busy to encourage preoccupation with the imponderable, and any problem that couldn't be solved would be either ignored or placed in the lap of the Almighty. And with the sunlight flickering on the flowery breakfast china she came to the same conclusion. She also remembered an allegedly true ghost story concerning a baronet who died a despotic and shambling octogenarian but returned to haunt his unfortunate heirs as he had been in his youth – slim and sprightly and much given to tumbling unsuspecting females.

Probably Jacob and Mary had died of natural causes in tranquil old age and had merely returned at this stage in their lives because it had been a particularly happy one. Why does one invariably attribute malignity and not benevolence to the incomprehensible, she wondered.

When breakfast was finished she rearranged the flowers in the sitting-room and then went upstairs to make her bed. In the bathroom there were signs that someone had taken a shower and she straightened the towels and twitched the waterproof curtains back in place with a triumphant little smile. She collected a few things for the washing machine, and meeting Mary at the foot of the stairs took her into the kitchen and showed her very slowly and patiently how the machine worked. ('Look – all you have to do is put the dirty clothes in *there*, put the soap powder in *there*, set the dial like *that*, and then switch on – it's really very easy . . .')

She returned to the sitting-room with a duster in her hand and was touched to see young Dorcas sitting alone on the sofa and frowning concentratedly at a copy of the *Radio Times*.

'Would you like to learn to read, Dorcas?'

The girl looked startled, as if she had been caught out in a misdemeanour, then nodded shyly.

91

'It's quite simple,' Eleanor said, 'once you know your letters.'

She went to the bureau and came back with some large sheets of paper and a felt-tipped pen. She sat down beside Dorcas, who shifted hastily when their knees touched.

'Now, the first letter of the alphabet is A,' Eleanor said, drawing. 'And A is for apple, for angel, for animal.' (And for automation, aviation and antibiotic, but we'll come to that later . . .) 'So can you draw me a nice A like that?'

She handed the pen to the girl, who took it doubtfully.

'That's right, but hold it lower down. Now, one stroke going there, and the next one starting from the same point and sloping out that way – that's it – and then a little bar across the middle. Well done, Dorcas!'

She looked up in time to see the girl's face and neck flush tender pink.

'Now comes the letter B. One stroke down, and then two half-circles at the side. And B stands for basket, for ball, and for brother . . . '

The girl copied each letter slowly and concentratedly, slipping into the role of pupil as easily as Eleanor returned to that of teacher. She wrote her name, breathing the letters and holding the pen so tightly that the blood drained from her fingers, and when Mary came into the room with the baby and told her to heed her brother she gave no more than an absent-minded nod.

They went through the alphabet again, the girl hesitant, but smiling a little now as she became increasingly affected by Eleanor's enthusiasm. Dithering between a P and an R she hit her forehead with her clenched fist, and when Eleanor in mock concern scrutinised her forehead for signs of injury she laughed aloud.

Then the baby began to cry. Still tightly swaddled despite the warmth of the day, it lay in the chair where Mary had left it, squirming to and fro like a fractious chrysalis while its reedy little voice imposed itself on the lesson and made concentration increasingly difficult. Murmuring an apology Dorcas left the sofa and picked the baby up. Jogging it to and fro she came back to Eleanor and they tried to continue the lesson. Mollified at first, the baby

92

ceased its struggling and its voice softened to a vague gurgling sound, but after a moment or two its sense of injury reasserted itself and its cries rose to new heights.

'Put him in the dining-room,' shouted Eleanor. 'All babies have to exercise their lungs at some time or other and he's interrupting the lesson.'

Dorcas obeyed, and Eleanor sat with her eyes closed as the noise diminished. She heard the dining-room door close, and after a moment or two became aware that Dorcas had reseated herself by her side.

'Now, where were we?'

'P - i - g is pig.'

'Correct. And now, how about dog?'

'Dog?'

'Think carefully now. D is the letter that comes after C, and do you remember how an O looks? It's a big round ball, isn't it, and it stands for orange. Have you ever seen an orange, Dorcas?'

The girl shook her head and then looked away, as if she were somehow at fault.

'I'm not sure when they were first introduced into this country but I've read about pomanders being made from oranges stuck with cloves and other spices to help ward off the awful smells—' She stopped. 'Sorry if I sound superior, but I suppose we've all become a bit too squeamish since the invention of modern drainage. But however different we may appear, Dorcas, we're exactly the same people, really. You mustn't ever forget that.'

Suddenly aware that the sound of crying had become louder again she looked up to see Jacob standing in the doorway with the baby dangling from under his arm. He strode across to the sofa and all but slung it at Dorcas, who scrambled to her feet in alarm.

'Did your mother not tell you to heed the nursling? Why then was it left to its own devices?'

With the baby clutched in her arms Dorcas bobbed a quick curtsy and then ducked aside as if she were expecting a blow.

'She was learning to read,' Eleanor said mildly.

'Reading is not for women. Theirs is the world of housewifery and of giving birth.'

'Oh, Jacob, you're so very—' She smiled. 'I was just going to say you're so very out of date.'

With his thumbs hooked in the top of his belt he stood staring at her defiantly. But somehow it seemed like the defiance of a child and she stared back at him calmly, aware that she was wiser by four hundred years.

'All right, Dorcas,' she said, without taking her eyes from his face, 'look after the baby while your mother is busy and we'll go on with the lesson this evening.'

Without haste she tidied the papers together and then walked past him into the garden.

Although she understood his jealous suspicion she was annoyed with him, and she busied herself with nipping off dead rose heads while she told herself that the sooner she got him involved in learning to read and write the better. Few men would be content to see their children outstrip them in any kind of endeavour and in Jacob she sensed an implacable resistance to any such thing. But he would have to be led, to be guided in such a way that he remained unaware of it, and she pictured his incredulous delight on the day when he realised that figures and letters made sense to him. She had never taught children of primary school age, but it seemed to her now that to unlock these first basic doors must be the most exciting and rewarding of all the many stages of education. She wondered whether there were any adult literacy classes run locally because she would rather like to help with them one day.

The early morning radiance had hardened, and the heat of the sun now seemed to bleach all colour from the garden. Wandering round the cottage to the kitchen she suddenly stopped short at the sight of Mary. With a plastic bucket balanced on a kitchen stool she was doing the washing, her bare arms rising and falling and the dirty soapless water slopping down the front of her skirt on to the grass. She was standing in full sunlight, with her hair tied back in a tea towel and her face pink with heat and exertion.

'Oh, *Mary*—' Eleanor hurried forward. 'What's wrong with the washing machine? I'd have helped if you didn't quite understand it – but even the sink would have been better than this!'

Mary smiled politely, evasively, and continued to pummel and scrub.

'There's lots of hot water in the kitchen; all you have to do is to turn on the tap.' Aware that annoyance was creeping into her voice she smiled and touched Mary gently on the shoulder.

'Did you hear me?'

'Yes, mistress.'

'Well, then . . .' She paused. 'Mary, you're not still frightened of me, are you?'

Mary stood motionless, her arms resting in the bucket and her face averted. In the sun's pitiless light she looked small and doomed and suddenly rather squalid, more like some nameless refugee than the rare miracle she undoubtedly was.

'Because there's nothing to be frightened of. I won't bite, you know . . .'

Mary remained mute, obviously waiting for her to go away, and Eleanor's annoyance suddenly swelled. Grasping her companion's arms she tried to remove them from the bucket in order to propel her towards the kitchen door. The bucket tilted, sloshing water over Eleanor's open sandals. Tight-lipped, Mary hung on, and with water oozing between her toes Eleanor released one of her arms in order to give it a sharp slap.

'For God's sake, Mary, stop being so damned *mulish!* Can't you see that I only want to help you?'

Shocked and very frightened Mary burst into tears, and appalled by her own stupidity Eleanor shoved the bucket out of the way and seized her in her arms. Holding her closely she stood rocking her against her shoulder while Mary emitted little shivering, sobbing moans.

'Oh my dear, why can't you trust me? I want to be friends, but you won't let me. Oh, you poor little wild bird of a woman, I'm so sorry . . .'

Once at school she had seized an insubordinate pupil by the shoulders and thrust her roughly outside the classroom door, and it had taken a long time to forget the rush of terrible savage pleasure as her fingers clamped hurtfully on

95

the yielding flesh. It had also taken a long while to re-establish the old trusting relationship between them, and she had vowed to herself that should her temper ever reach snapping point again she would walk out of the room for the few minutes necessary to regain self-control.

'Let's be friends, Mary. Let's learn to talk and laugh together, and if there's anything that worries you or frightens you, all you have to do is to tell me and I'll do everything within my power to help and explain. So promise you'll come to me, there's a good girl . . .'

Mary made what seemed like a little fumbling movement of acquiescence and Eleanor was on the point of releasing her in order to retrieve the washing from the overturned bucket when the sudden tinkle of falling glass made her look up sharply.

One of the two older boys – Ned, she thought – was up at the bedroom window, brandishing something in his hand and sniggering.

'Your windows have the real glass then, mistress,' he called down to her. 'Real glass like in churches and palaces —' From somewhere in the room behind him came the sound of muffled laughter.

'Come down from there,' she ordered, then recognised the object that he was holding. It was one of her shoes.

'Real glass like the gentry do have,' he said, and tapped the high heel experimentally against another of the panes. It too shattered, and fell on to the paving below.

'Ned – come down at once!' Letting go of Mary Eleanor went closer to the cottage and stood looking up at him sternly. 'You have no right to touch my things and certainly no right to deliberately break windows. So I suggest you come downstairs at once and apologise!'

He remained where he was, the shoe upraised in his fist, and for the first time she found herself having to face the fact of his awful and implacable oafishness. Like a round pink vegetable his face peered down at her from its frame of crisp Liberty curtaining, and after a brief glance at Mary who was slowly wringing out the upset washing, Eleanor marched in through the kitchen and made for the staircase.

A crash of feet forestalled her as both William and Ned

hurtled down, leaping the last six stairs and knocking Mo's portrait crooked before escaping into the garden from the front door. In silence she straightened the picture while she listened to the sound of their guffaws retreating through the garden and out into the lane. Standing by the front door she saw one of the smaller girls arranging a little circle of pebbles at the side of the path, and although she glanced up at the disturbance her face remained impassive. Idiotically Eleanor had half-hoped that it might display a modicum of sympathy.

She went back into the cottage, and walking through the sitting-room became aware of Jacob lying full-length on the sofa, a bunch of cushions under his head. There was cunning in the sliver of eye which followed her.

'Jacob, I do think you could teach your sons a few manners.'

'They have manners enough for their place in life, mistress.' He recomposed himself for sleep.

'And you've apparently nothing better to do than to sprawl with your feet on the furniture,' she added.

The room seemed to have developed a frowsy, untidy look and the air smelt stale. She walked round it, picking up the bright toys they had bought on the previous day, aware that the children appeared to have forsaken them in favour of more elemental things such as pebbles and sticks and – her lips tightened – the simple fun of breaking windows. She heaped the toys in a corner and pushed the chairs back into their rightful places, frowning and rubbing her hand over the dirty marks that had appeared on one of them.

'I take my ease because all the work has been done,' Jacob said with his eyes closed. 'The fields are tended and there is no livestock to feed. The water is drawn and the buttery is stocked with food which has seen no man's hand in its creation. So what is there for men to do in your world, mistress, but scratch themselves and go to sleep?'

'They read newspapers, write letters, keep accounts, take an intelligent interest in the world outside. Life for us now is no longer a matter of physical toil alternating with sleep.'

'Those are skills of which I have no knowledge.'

'You could learn,' Eleanor said. 'The same as your daughter.'

She continued to tidy the room, moving to and fro past the sofa without looking at him.

'You would have me sit down with a lesson book next to my own child?'

'Why not? You could help one another.'

He made no reply, but she sensed his opposition.

'Listen, Jacob.' She sat down facing the sofa with her hands clasped round her knees. 'It's time we started thinking seriously about what's going to happen to you all. I know that we didn't exactly arrange your return here, and that we must be prepared for the fact that you might all go – go away again just as suddenly as you arrived, but in the meantime we've got to follow some sort of plan which will help you and your family to adjust and become integrated in the modern world.' She paused, but he made no comment.

'I don't want to tell other people about you yet. It's too soon, and I'm certain that it would only lead to disaster. The press would be down here in a flash, and instead of treating the situation intelligently they'd merely sensationalise the whole thing. They'd cast me as some kind of mad clairvoyant and they'd only succeed in confusing and frightening you and your family, so my idea is this, Jacob. Stay here quietly, all of you, until you have mastered a few of the basic skills like reading and writing and coming up to date with history and geography. I could teach you – teaching is my profession – and then when you feel sufficiently confident to mix socially with ordinary people, we can consider the next step to take. For one of the most significant facts of contemporary life is that everyone has to work for his living. Ultimately you will have to work for yours too, Jacob, if only because I haven't enough money of my own to keep you all.'

She unclasped her hands and sat looking at him expectantly. His eyes were still closed and his mouth seemed to be smiling faintly, then she realised that the quiet bee-like buzzing she could hear was the beginning of a snore. Abruptly she got up and left the room.

6

At half past eleven that morning Eric Seward became suddenly aware of the perfect excuse to return to Jackdaw's Cottage: he had left his hat there. Sitting at his desk he remembered with absolute clarity having dropped it down by his chair as he sat in that marvellous golden room sipping sherry with Eleanor Millard.

He decided to ring her up and ask whether he could call in one evening to pick it up, then changed his mind when he realised that she might offer to leave it at the Record Office for him, to save him the bother. He didn't want that to happen. He wanted to see her again in her own setting, to sit with her in the gracious quiet of that small, ancient building on the edge of its corn-filled valley. Like an invalid in search of a better climate he had become increasingly certain that another visit would have a beneficial effect on his troubles, and he was now more convinced than ever that Eleanor possessed the precise blend of sympathy, amity and brisk common sense of which he was in such need.

Corinne had not returned last night. At breakfast the children had seemed pale and listless and disinclined to eat, but having established that their temperatures were normal he had taken them off to school because they were too young to stay at home by themselves. Before going to the office he had put their sheets and nightclothes in the washing machine and had phoned Corinne's mother to ask whether she would meet the children after school. She said that she didn't normally go out in hot weather, but supposed she had better try. He thanked her, plastered two slices of bread with meat paste, made a flask of coffee and hurried away.

The office was quiet, at least his part of it was. One of the big tables was filled with uniformed 0-level students researching the cloth trade in Hanoverian England and over in the corner was an American septuagenarian hungrily tracing her family tree. Everyone needs to belong somewhere, he thought. No matter how invincible we think we are, we all need to derive strength from the knowledge that we have our own rightful place on some little patch or other. I wish my little patch were Jackdaw's Cottage and that Eleanor Millard was –

The telephone rang at his elbow. 'Call for you.'

'Hello?'

'Mr Seward? Mr Eric Seward? The County Hospital here. Your wife, a Mrs Corinne Margaret Seward, has been brought into Casualty suffering from shock and we understand that she has been involved in a car accident. Perhaps you could call here as soon as possible and ask for Doctor Chowd at the reception desk. Her condition is not serious.'

He got up slowly, and stood blinking down at his desk and arranging his pens and pencils in a neat row. And the only thing he could think of was that this might well prevent him from calling on Eleanor Millard later that evening.

Inventing a brief excuse for his absence he slipped out of the office and made for the car park.

Doctor Chowd was not available when he enquired, but a nurse showed him the way to the casualty room and he found Corinne lying on a sort of couch behind a screen. Two-thirds of her was covered by a red blanket and the part that was visible looked distinctly unsavoury. She had a black eye, a strip of sticking plaster on her cheek and her hair looked like coconut matting. Seeing him she made a half-hearted attempt to raise herself on one elbow, swore, then collapsed again.

He found it difficult to say anything. 'Hello, Corinne.'

'Uh-huh.'

'What happened?'

'The party got rough.'

'Not for the first time.'

'Oh, shut up,' she said through cracked lips.

He supposed that he should call her a bloody fool and a God-awful mother to his children, but he didn't seem to have the energy. In any case she already knew. She lay back with one grubby forearm hiding her face from the bright lights while he continued to stand there with the patient, rather empty expression of someone waiting for a bus.

'What sort of accident was it?' he asked finally.

'We were going over to Phyl's place in Poppy's car and hit a lamp post.'

He had never heard of Poppy and had no means of knowing whether Phyl was male or female. 'But no one was seriously hurt?'

'Think the chap who was driving was. He was high, so they'll do him for dangerous driving.'

'Does it bother you?'

She remained silent for a moment, then said: 'Why should it? I never met him before.'

He was about to turn away when a small brown-skinned man in a white coat came round the screen. 'Hello, Mrs Seward, how are we now? Feeling better?'

He removed her arm from across her face, prised open the undamaged eye and peered inside for a moment before letting it fall shut again. He took her pulse.

'Nothing much wrong except for a few little bumps and bruises, so I think home is the best place for you.'

'Home?' said Eric involuntarily and the doctor turned to him for the first time. 'And you are Mr Seward? Perhaps we can have a little word about this . . .'

Without speaking Eric followed him into the corridor. They stood in a corner by a fire extinguisher while the life of the hospital flowed busily past.

'You really feel that she's fit enough to come home?'

Doctor Chowd eyed him beadily. 'Her injuries are superficial but she has other problems which need urgent attention, Mr Seward. Why is she living like this? Why is she drinking and taking drugs? I think you must ask yourself this urgently because she is a nice young woman, very graceful and charming, and maybe it is your fault—'

'How she behaves is nothing to do with me,' Eric said. 'God knows I've tried—'

'Nothing to do with you?' repeated Doctor Chowd. He began to speak softly and very rapidly. 'It is everything to do with you. You are her husband and so it is time to ask yourself some questions. Do you neglect her, forget to praise her? Are you too busy with your own affairs to notice that she is having to seek attention elsewhere, Mr Seward? Do you go out on expense account lunches and then drink beer with your work friends in the evenings? Are you sexually adequate, Mr Seward? Ask yourself now, are you capable of pleasing your wife in the bedroom, because contrary to old ideas women are highly—'

'You said she could come home,' Eric said woodenly. 'Do you mean right now?'

'I mean right now, Mr Seward. And I suggest that you give her a nice bath and a nice meal and then go to bed with her. Talk with her, Mr Seward. Find out what it is she is lacking, and in what way you are to blame, and then perhaps—' The small wired instrument protruding from his breast pocket began to emit a high bleeping sound. 'That is all for now, Mr Seward. Think over what I have said and remember that many men, many *many* men would envy you with such a charming and graceful young wife . . .' He hurried away.

Left to himself Eric leaned against the fire extinguisher feeling sullen and mutinous. For a moment he considered walking out and leaving Corinne to find her own way home – if to come home was her intention – then he looked up and saw her. Leaning on the arm of a nurse she was walking slowly and jerkily with her head bent, and something about her demeanour reminded him of the terrible hang-dog shuffling of a down-and-out. Stiff-faced he went towards her and the nurse placed Corinne's inert arm within his as if she were bestowing upon him some treasure of infinite worth.

He drove slowly, conscious of her presence and thinking that the only sensible piece of advice the doctor had given was that she should have a bath. They reached the house without speaking, and although he leaned across and opened her door he left her to get out of the car on her own. The place smelt of chips, and looked dreary with dead flies on the window-ledges and bits of washing hung round the kitchen.

'Do you want a cup of tea or something?'

102

She shook her head, leaning against the wall and shivering. She was wearing jeans and a grubby tee-shirt with *I like it!* written across the front and she looked more like a drop-out student than a wife and mother of two.

'What are you going to do now, then?'

'I don't know.'

'Well, I've got to get back to the office.'

'Okay . . .'

She turned away and he knew that she was crying. So let her get on with it. Do her good. But instead, he put out his hand and touched the awful coconut matting hair and said: 'Don't cry, love.'

She grabbed at his hand, holding it and squeezing it, and her face was blind and stupid with tears. Childlike, she kept trying to talk through the sobs that tore at her and he found himself holding her in his arms, breathing in the smell of sweat and dirt and marijuana and telling her brokenly that he loved her.

'Don't ever leave me again – I can't stand it . . .'

'I won't – I won't. But don't you ever leave *me* . . .'

'I don't. I never would . . .'

'You do mentally. I can't follow . . .'

'Then we must make a solemn promise never to leave one another in any sort of way, except for me going to the office—'

'I want to come with you—'

'Okay, be a typist—'

'Oh God, I feel so ill and so awful . . .'

'Come along,' he said, leading her gently. 'The first thing is to have a bath and then some nice supper, and then what about beddy-byes?'

'You'll come too?' She paused to look at him with her one good eye, the other a wet and lurid sunset of black and blue and greeny-yellow. The sticking plaster hung down disclosing a bright red gash, and her nose was running.

'Where else would I go?' he said. 'Oh, my little heart's love, where else?'

Having gathered for a light lunch of salad, biscuits and cheese the family at Jackdaw's Cottage had dispersed again. Mary was up in the bedroom with the baby, Jacob was squatting in the front doorway idly whittling a bit of wood with a kitchen knife and from somewhere deep in the garden came the murmur of children chanting, a drowsy, peaceful sound like the crooling of pigeons. A lot of the games the younger ones played seemed to involve the singing or chanting of incantations, and with their permission Eleanor proposed to make a note of the words and learn the various meanings of the games involved.

But now she was going down to the farm to fetch the milk and collect the mail and the daily paper.

She felt tired and a little depressed, and walking down the path to the front gate told herself that, like the plants, she would feel better when it rained. But in the meantime, she would water the garden tonight no matter what happened.

She was just getting into the car when the two older boys appeared, sidling out of the hedge and grinning at her appeasingly.

'Is it allowed that we come along of you, mistress?'

'Happen we can come in the cart-thing too?'

'No,' Eleanor said shortly. 'I'm not pleased with you.'

'What must we do to please then, mistress?' asked the one called Will, and despite his air of humble abasement she caught the quick smirk that passed between them.

'You can start by behaving yourselves. And by that I mean leaving other people's property alone, not breaking things—'

'This is our property,' Ned said very quietly. He pulled his forelock. 'This dwelling belongs to my father.'

So it's come at last, she thought. If only from the children.

'Whether the house belongs legally to your father or to me is far too complicated a problem for any of us to solve at the moment, and the situation is entirely dependent on our mutual goodwill and determination to live together happily and at peace. But when it comes to things *inside* the house I have no hesitation in claiming them as my own, and I'm afraid that both you and the rest of your family have no option but to accept them as such.'

She heard herself speaking in the slow, quiet, well-

104

modulated tones of school, stressing the key words and laying additional emphasis every now and then by a slight nod of the head. She sat down in the driving seat and closed the door, rolling down the window because of the heat.

They came closer, their round turnip faces beseeching.

'If you please, mistress—'

'We will promise to serve you well, mistress, if we may ride with you in the cart—'

'It isn't a cart, it's a *car*,' she said, starting the engine and feeling a certain rather mean pleasure when they jumped hastily back. 'Behave yourselves properly for two days and I will take you for a ride *then*, but not *before*.'

Reversing with swift competence she bumped away down the lane.

She found Mrs Lacey in the kitchen, slapping plimsoll-shod round the stone floor from one task to another. It was an old room, with heavy black beams and a big oak table covered in tartan plastic. A black cat was sitting on one corner with its feet tucked under it, and it rose politely as Eleanor crossed the threshold. She went over to it and tickled its neck.

'Here we are, Mrs Millard.' Mrs Lacey handed her the milk and a folded newspaper. 'No post today. Lovely weather still, isn't it? The corn's coming on a treat.'

Eleanor agreed, then asked whether she could spare her some extra milk.

'How many? One?'

'Could you manage four?'

'Four pints extra?' said Mrs Lacey, intrigued. 'Well, I daresay I could, what with the girl down at her auntie's and the boy off on the school trip.'

'Then perhaps I could order some more for tomorrow, and include your four pints. Which would make eight in all.'

'Got comp'ny up there, have you?'

'Yes,' said Eleanor. She smiled, then bent her head over the cat which had rolled over on its back. Mrs Lacey went back to the fridge.

'Was going to have to make a blancmange, but now you've saved me the trouble. Here you are then, four pints

105

– and four pints again tomorrow, you say?'

'That's it,' said Eleanor. 'Many thanks, Mrs Lacey.'

'Staying long, are they?'

'I'm not really sure. I mean, nothing's been planned yet . . .' Eleanor felt that she must be sounding evasive, but Mrs Lacey appeared not to notice anything unusual. She leaned back against the table with her arms folded across her front.

'Well, I'm glad to think you've got a bit of comp'ny. Me and Dad often talk about you all alone up there. I mean, having a nice ole place is all very well, but you can't talk to it, can you?'

Eleanor agreed that you couldn't and began to pick up the bottles of milk but Mrs Lacey forestalled her, slapping across to the dresser and extracting a plastic carrier bag from the pile of other things lying there.

'Got kiddies staying, have you?'

'Yes,' said Eleanor. 'With their parents.'

'Oh, how nice! Funny, we thought we heard some young voices from up the lane yesterday.' She placed the bottles in the carrier bag while Eleanor held it open. 'I love kiddies, myself. They make a place come alive so, don't they?'

Eleanor nodded, smiling, and when the carrier was loaded put the newspaper under her arm and began to walk towards the open door. Mrs Lacey accompanied her.

'Just had one of our young pigs stole. Dad reckons it's them ole gyppos – there's a new lot of them camped down by Bell's Wood.'

'Oh dear, I am sorry.'

They walked together across the sun-baked farmyard towards Eleanor's car.

'Poor ole sow over there looking all over about for her little pig . . . it was gyppos who broke in the post office up Wendon Green the other week. Stole three pounds seventy out the Spastics' tin . . .'

'How dreadful,' murmured Eleanor. She placed the carrier bag carefully on the back seat. 'Thank you so much, Mrs Lacey, and if I could have four pints again tomorrow – plus the four I owe you—'

'Send some of the kiddies down to collect it!' chirped Mrs

106

Lacey. 'They could see Spot's new puppies – got eight out in the barn and kiddies always love animals, don't they?'

When Eleanor reached home the cottage seemed as quiet as when she had left it, and only a furtive rustling in the hedge made her pause for a moment as she got out of the car. Gathering up the milk and the newspaper she went indoors, noticing Jacob's piece of wood and the kitchen knife lying discarded on the front door step. Jacob himself she found outstretched and snoring on the sitting-room sofa. She left him to it.

Alone in the kitchen she stowed the milk in the fridge and then stood looking round. It seemed dirty and untidy, with solidified fat splashes on the hob unit and scrumpled tea towels lying around. Crumbs littered the floor and flies buzzed among the dirty plates on the table and draining-boards. But there was something else about it too; leaning against the door of the fridge she had a strange and indefinable impression tha⁺ the place was in the process of undergoing some kind of elemental change. The crispness, the sharp and shining edges of the technological age were being stealthily eroded by another influence.

Her gaze rested on the jug of weeds that stood on the table among the unwashed plates; with the garden full of roses and, come to that, the lane full of wild flowers, the coarse leaves bunched carelessly together seemed a strange idea of decoration. Moving closer she recognised nettles and docks, and began to realise with a slight sense of chill that they were probably medicinal herbs waiting to be made into potions or possets, ointments or unguents. In all probability they trusted her ideas on medicine as little as she trusted theirs.

But there were other things. Some small animal bones, possibly those of a stoat or a weasel, lay carefully arranged on a Pyrex dish. Bleached and polished, they looked as if they had been found in a field and brought home as something of particular significance. She hesitated to disturb them. And although her own kitchen friends were still present, the blender, the toaster, the plate-warmer, the electric skillet, all of them waiting merely for the touch of her finger to spring into life, she felt an additional twinge of disquiet when close to the electric coffee grinder she noticed a number of beans which had spilled out on to the Formica worktop. Someone had carefully arranged them in the shape of a cross.

Abruptly she decided that she was not going to wash up. Instead, she closed the door behind her and returned to the sitting-room. Unfolding the newspaper she sat down in an armchair and read. Jacob's snoring had increased from a buzzing to a raucous rattling, and Eleanor was on the point of expostulating when a sudden and far more terrible sound tore through the room.

Rigid, she heard the roar of a car's engine, the scream of gears in agonised conflict and then a loud crash. Leaping to her feet she rushed out into the garden. Outside the gate her car lay on its side in the ditch, the windscreen shattered and the wheels still revolving. Will and Ned were in the act of scrambling out of it and bolting into the hedgerow.

Shocked and distraught she stumbled towards it, the brambles ripping her skirt, for in those confused first moments the car seemed like a living creature in pain. Scratched and breathless she caught the upturned front wheel in her hands and stopped its spinning, but there was nothing practical she could do and when strong hands took her by the shoulders and helped her up from the ditch she found herself shaking with rage.

'Those two *damned* sons of yours!'

'As God's my judge, they'll rue this day,' Jacob said, releasing her. 'Go to the house, mistress, while I set about some work.'

Gently he propelled her towards the gate, where Mary and Dorcas and the two younger children were standing in a group. Without speaking they made way for her.

'I'll have to ring the garage to send someone out,' Eleanor muttered as she passed them.

Alone in the sitting-room she paced up and down for a moment, trying to calm herself, then went over to the phone. Checking the number she dialled it, then replaced the receiver with a curse. The line was engaged. She recommenced her pacing, then stopped abruptly as the silence was split by hoarse screams of pain accompanied by the sound of heavy rhythmical blows. She listened to the sounds increasing both in savagery and in torment, then, sickened, clapped her hands over her ears and closed her eyes.

Tears ran down her cheeks, and for the first time she wished with all her strength that the Dawes had never returned.

III
THE FINISH

1

With a little punnet of raspberries for Mr Dainton and two freshly pulled lettuces for Mrs Millard in her bicycle basket, the vicar's wife mounted the saddle and rode off, tinkling her bell.

The afternoon seemed to her a little less hot than yesterday and she welcomed the light breeze that played against her forehead and flapped languidly at her skirt. Bowling down the quiet road from the vicarage she mentally checked through the notes for the parish mag that were folded in her handbag. Mr Dainton, as editor, always liked to receive his material by the twenty-seventh of the month at the very latest and here we were, already at the twenty-fifth. Heavens, how time flew.

The Gardening Notes, Miss Salmon's WI entry, the account of the British Legion's outing to Windsor and a note to record the passing away of poor old Mrs Agnew *(who will be sadly missed by us all)*. Sally Burton's baby was already five days overdue so it would have to wait now until the August issue. Nothing more to come, she thought contentedly, except for the possibility of some last-minute event, but July was invariably a quiet month in the parish. A sparrowhawk flew up from the wide grass verge with a small rodent in its talons and Mrs Parsloe wobbled slightly as she watched its progress.

There was little traffic on the road and she waved to a tractor driver before turning down the lane that led to Great Brissets. She had decided to take the long way round to Mr Dainton's house because she enjoyed a cycle ride, and she looked with glowing pleasure at the rolling fields on either side, all of them bearing a full burden of tall ripening corn.

'We thank Thee, Heavenly Father,' she said aloud, 'for

the glorious bounty of Thy love . . .'

Two miles from the vicarage and more than three from Mr Dainton's she became aware of a bumping sensation beneath the saddle and, dismounting, saw with dismay that her back tyre was flat. Propping the bicycle against a farm gate she pumped it up, and heard the air escaping again almost as fast. Peering closely, she discovered a sizeable slit in it.

Slowly she replaced the pump and stood considering. Three miles was a long way to walk when she could dictate the parish mag entries over the phone, and Mrs Millard's cottage was at least another two miles further on. The exertion of pumping the tyre had made her feel hot, so reluctantly she turned the bicycle round and began to walk back the way she had come. Nothing passed her on the way, and by the time she reached the vicarage she felt very tired.

'Arthur – my dear, I had a puncture,' she called as she walked through to the dishevelled sitting-room. He wasn't there. Neither was he in his study, or in the kitchen making a cup of tea.

She walked out into the tangled garden, the sun hitting her temples, and despite her tiredness the need to tell Arthur about the puncture increased. She called him, and somnolent birds flew up among the leaves, annoyed by the disturbance. She followed the roughly mown path to the churchyard and then entered the church, the big iron handle clanging.

She found him in one of the front pews, bent over with his forehead almost touching the hymnbook ledge, and at first she thought that he was praying. She stood waiting deferentially, then something about his continued stillness began to alarm her. She moved forward, calling his name and putting her hand on his bowed shoulder. She became aware that he was breathing, but his eyes were closed and in spite of the cool of the church his forehead was bathed in sweat.

'My dear, you're ill . . .' She put her arm round him and sank down on to the pew beside him. She looked at him closely, anxiously, and then recoiled as the smell of his breath reached her.

114

'Arthur,' she said uncertainly.

He opened his eyes very slowly and turned his face towards her. He stared at her glassily. 'God and evil are synonymous,' he said.

She gazed back at him in the stream of tinted light coming through the east window, taking in the ashen face and the weary haggard eyes. The smell of his breath was very strong.

'Arthur—' she said in amazement. 'Good heavens, Arthur, I do believe you're drunk.'

Sweeping a clear space on one of the worktops Eleanor removed a leg of lamb from the fridge. She had washed the dishes and given the kitchen a superficial clean and was in the act of switching on the oven when Jacob came in. He walked over to her, and putting one hand on her waist reached up and switched it off again. She remained motionless, soberly contemplating him.

He was wearing his twentieth-century clothes with a casual ease now, and although there were food stains on his flowered shirt his thick bob of hair was brushed and his teeth were clean. He remained close, with his hand on her waist, and his manner towards her she could only describe to herself as one of kindliness born of self-confidence.

'Turn and turn about, mistress,' he said. 'Tonight Mary and I will prepare the meal and you shall sup with us.'

'Oh no, really . . .' She wanted to move away from him but a strange lassitude prevented her.

'Oh *yea*, mistress.' He raised a blunt forefinger and gently tapped her on the nose with it. 'The woman and I will take much delight in asking you to share with us the Feast of St James, and the children shall help in its preparation.'

'Is it really the Feast of St James?'

'If it was *really* the twenty-fourth day of July yesterday,' he replied mockingly.

'I told you it was.'

'So be it then.' He released her and went over to the window.

'And the year,' Eleanor said carefully, 'is 1981.'

He stared out across the slope of the garden to the fields

115

beyond. 'The twenty-fifth day of July, when the weather is sweet and the corn is turning, and when men and women can beguile themselves for an hour or two before harvest work sets in, breaking their backs and flaying their hands and burning their skins to clay . . . '

Yesterday she would have wanted to hear more; to have stood quietly by while she tried to absorb the thoughts and the choice of words of this miraculous man from the past, but now practicalities intervened.

'Are you quite sure you know how to use the oven, and everything?'

He turned from the window and stared hard at her. 'I always put to good account everything that comes to my hand, mistress.'

He walked over to her again, and without haste kissed her on the mouth. She stood there for a moment, limp and compliant, then pushed him away.

'I don't think that was very wise of you, Jacob.'

'But madam, you have a careworn look. Why do you not go to your bed and rest while the feast is prepared?'

'No, I must help see to things . . .' She looked round the kitchen.

'Such things as are needful the woman and I answer for. You are tired, and when the feast is prepared I will wake you.'

'I'm not tired, I've just got a headache . . .' She found herself weakening. Already the day seemed to have been too long, and she had a sudden parched need for solitude. 'Well, if it's really what you want, and you're absolutely sure you can manage, there's the joint of lamb. I generally start if off at about four hundred degrees – there on the dial, look – so switch the oven on and don't forget to wait until the little red light goes off. That means that it's reached the correct temperature—'

'To your bed, mistress.'

'I think Mary knows where the potatoes and vegetables are kept . . .'

'All shall be reckoned with.'

'Oh, and there's a big blackcurrant pie that should come out of the freezer soon . . . you'll recognise it, Jacob, by the picture of blackcurrants on top . . .'

He took her arm and guided her out of the kitchen towards the staircase. Sighing and rubbing her forehead she went up to her room while he stood watching with a smile in his eyes.

It seemed airless under the hot tiles and she filled the washbasin with cold water and then lowered her face into it for a moment. She splashed her forearms, and then stood slowly drying herself and stroking the wet strands of hair back from her forehead. Still not certain that it had been wise to allow them the freedom of the kitchen, she took two aspirin and told herself that twenty minutes' rest would make her feel better and still give her time to superintend the cooking of supper. It had been very nice of Jacob to suggest preparing the meal in her absence and to refuse his offer would be tactless in the extreme. Turning back the counterpane she kicked off her sandals and lay down. The relief seemed instantaneous, and she floated in sleep while the murmur of children's voices drifted harmoniously through the open window.

Yet her mind refused to surrender itself wholly and the afternoon's events returned, flitting behind her closed eyes like a jerky and distorted newsreel. She heard her own voice telling the two boys that she would not take them for a ride in the car: *I'm not pleased with you . . . you must learn to leave other people's property alone and not break things . . .* The voice sounded thin and prim, with a peevish, petulant note. The voice of a desiccated schoolmarm. She shifted restlessly, moaning a little at the noise of the car as it crashed into the ditch, and the screams of the boys being thrashed by Jacob rang in her head so loudly that it seemed as if it must be happening all over again. Confusedly she propped herself up on her elbow, and for a moment was certain that the two voices screaming in her head had been joined by a third, even higher and more desperate. Then she slid down again, the pillow cool against her cheek, and the weight of sleep when it came was such that she remained undisturbed by the rhythmical sound of chopping that came from outside the front hedge.

Everything would be all right, and if they couldn't

117

remember how to put the oven on they would call her.

'And tell me, pray, what has God ever done for me?'

The Reverend Parsloe was still in the church pew, but instead of leaning over the hymnbook rest he was now sitting propped against the far end with his feet on the seat and his ankles crossed, and his manner, now that he was awake, was one of bleary-eyed truculence. Mrs Parsloe was sitting in the pew behind with her hands clasped under her chin.

'God has done a great deal for you, Arthur,' she said. 'He has bestowed upon you many wonderful gifts.'

'Name one.'

Fighting an impulse to say *What about me?* she looked briefly at the hammerbeam roof and replied: 'Good health.'

The vicar snorted.

'He gave you good health, and it would be very ungrateful to squander it by – by doing what you were doing this afternoon.'

The shock of her discovery had not yet faded, and there had been insufficient time to examine her reactions. Pity, she supposed, and perturbation, plus a simple desire to feel cross with him for being so silly. 'Let's go home and have some tea,' she added. 'I've had a puncture and I feel rather tired.'

But the vicar shuffled into a more comfortable position and said: 'Listen, God doesn't give two damns whether I get pissed as a newt daily. He doesn't care whether I drop down dead. He doesn't care whether everyone on this planet drops down dead. He's just an acidulated old cynic, and I suppose that makes two of us.'

His words distressed her more profoundly than his intoxication until it occurred to her that he would never say such things if he were sober. Blasphemy and drunkenness were obviously closely allied, and both were symptoms in Arthur's case of some sort of spiritual malaise.

'My dear, you're talking wildly and for effect,' she admonished him. 'The real fact is that you are ill, Arthur. One cannot deny that a pastoral calling no longer involves

118

the work that it did, but you have taken the changing times in which we live as a personal insult. You are still needed by God.'

'Let's leave Him out of it. Who else needs me? My parishioners?'

To insist, in spite of all the evidence to the contrary, that he was indispensable to his parishioners would have been foolish, and Mrs Parsloe was not a foolish woman.

'I need you, Arthur,' she said, gently touching his arm.

He looked at her sourly. 'In that case I presume you're willing to accompany me when I leave here.'

Striving to absorb this additional shock without trace, she said as mildly as possible: 'Are you really thinking of leaving the parish? How very sad. We've been here for a long time now, and I'm—'

'Just like everyone else, you're obsessed by the past. Having been in one place for a long while is more than adequate reason for staying there until you die, even if you don't like it.'

'But I *do* like it.'

'But can't you see, it's a void – it's a void!' His voice rose in an uncontrollable shriek that rang through the church. 'And if you haven't got a mouldering moth-eaten past of your own you try to crawl into someone else's like a maggot in a lump of cheese. And like that fool woman who was here the other day—'

Soothingly she patted his sleeve. 'If you want to ask the bishop for a transfer to an urban parish of course I'll agree. It's only a matter of adjusting one's life a little . . .'

'When I go to see the bishop,' he bared his large crooked teeth in a grin that made her recoil, 'it will be to hand in my resignation as a parish priest. I'm leaving the ministry, forgetting all about the cure of souls, and I'm going to work for someone a little less removed, a little less chill and impartial and blandly, bloodily indifferent than the Bloke up there.' He jabbed his finger heavenwards and his wife gave a little cry.

'Arthur, this is terrible blasphemy—'

'Neither am I going to spend any more of my time waiting to be needed, to be consulted or approached by even one of the eight hundred and seventy-nine souls in my so-called pastoral care. If any one of them should suddenly evince a mad desire to be christened, married or buried by me – too bad. They've had their chips. I'm going off to work for a more practical organisation—'

'Have you a particular one in mind?'

'Kent County Council. I'm going to be a deckchair attendant on Margate sands. And in the winter months I shall be self-employed, trundling round the streets grinding scissors—'

'*Arthur!*' Mrs Parsloe said very loudly and suddenly. '*Listen* to me. I can forgive the dreadful things you have said because I know that you are tipsy, but I'm not sure yet whether I can forgive the feebleness of spirit that has impelled you to *get* tipsy. We shall have to see. Because if there's one thing I find hard to swallow it's self-pity, and I never thought that you – you, of all people – would ever succumb to it. If rural parish life isn't sufficiently stimulating then by all means arrange a transfer with the diocesan bishop. Ask for a living in one of the distressed areas in Liverpool or Glasgow. Try the dockland areas, or one of the new concrete jungles where people mug each other, commit rape and murder just because they too are filled with hate and self-pity. If you decide to do that, Arthur, I will come with you. I will stand shoulder to shoulder with you, work by your side and support you in every way that I can. But if you are seriously determined to leave the ministry simply because you no longer have an awed and loving congregation gazing up at you and hanging on your every word at morning service every Sunday, then it's no good. I don't want to know. You can go off and drop out and do something ridiculous like selling deckchair tickets all on your own and – and the best of British luck to you!'

The tears which she had been fighting suddenly burst forth; coughing and hiccoughing wildly she sat gazing at the altar through a scalding, shimmering haze, and the majestic light flooding through the east window revealed her blotched, creased face with its red nose and contorted mouth in all its elderly agony. The Reverend Parsloe sat staring at her in bleary astonishment, and in an excess of

120

baffled fury she raised the hand that had been stroking his sleeve and hit him. The blow landed on his mouth and she felt the hardness of teeth against her knuckles.

'Bunty!'

'Don't Bunty me!' she cried, and then began to laugh hysterically. The sound of it ran crazily round the church, and the realisation that they had chosen the house of God as a setting for the first major row in all their married life appalled and scandalised yet failed to calm her. With her hands over her face she rushed out of the pew and collided noisily with the font before stumbling out into the churchyard.

2

Daylight had faded from the bedroom when Eleanor awoke. Having slept with unusual soundness she woke slowly and lay wondering what time it was and why she had gone to sleep in the first place. Then she remembered her headache, and Jacob's insistence that she was to be his and Mary's guest for supper. She could hear the murmur of voices downstairs and the occasional clink of cooking pans and she switched on the bedside lamp, screwing up her eyes to see the time. To her surprise it was almost seven-thirty. She got up, hurriedly groping for her sandals, then opened the bedroom door and peered out. The sounds of preparation were louder now and her nostrils caught the agreeable scent of roasting meat.

Smiling, she went back into the bedroom and began to comb her hair, then as an afterthought decided to change her dress. She selected a loose Indian cotton one that Mo had always liked, smoothed on some make-up and arranged her hair in a loose chignon. Before leaving the room she plumped up her pillows and replaced the counterpane, meticulously smoothing the wrinkles. Everything was neat and tidy, and she looked round with satisfaction before closing the door.

Halfway downstairs her smile vanished and she stood rigid with shock.

A huge fire was burning in the sitting-room fireplace, in the centre of which a young pig hung suspended by its four feet. Fat was dripping into the red heart of the fire and the boy Will was crouched on a stool, basting the carcass and shielding his stinging eyes from the heat and smoke.

Dazedly she saw that the dining table had been dragged through from the other room and was now drawn up before the fire. Mary, with her head shrouded in a tea towel, was stirring a hot saucepan on the polished wood while Dorcas, equally absorbed, was slicing rough chunks of bread on it.

For a moment or two it seemed as if Eleanor were incapable of any further movement; then with an anguished cry she darted into the room, rushing first to the fire then abruptly changing direction as Mary dragged the saucepan across the table with a loud rasping sound. Wheeling suddenly she almost collided with Jacob, who had just come in through the front door with a pile of logs in his arms. He greeted her cheerily.

'How now, my good mistress? Welcome to the Feast of St James—'

'What on earth possessed you to light a fire in here? And that pig – where did you . . . Oh, my God, just look at all the mess!'

Distraught, she continued to run from one precious object to another, and when she had finished stamping out sparks on the pale yellow carpet her eyes caught the pile of logs which Jacob was about to precipitate between the armchair and the drinks table.

'Those logs – where did you get them? Oh, *no!*' She rushed to the window and looked out, then sped to the telephone and picked up the receiver. It was dead.

'You forbore to tell us of the tall naked trees grown for kindling,' Jacob said. 'Truly, yours is a world of miracles.'

'That tree happened to be a thing called a telegraph pole, which is our means of – Oh, never mind.'

'And now we will give you the taste of fresh and lusty meat killed not an hour since,' Jacob went on, apparently unaware of her agitation. 'Do you fancy it's near cooked, boy?'

He took a long cooking fork from Will and prodded the pig. Juices spurted and fell back into the flames with a hiss. In the livid firelight his face had assumed a look of sensuous gluttony and abruptly Eleanor remembered the screaming she had heard in – or maybe outside – her dream.

'Where did you get that pig?' She stood with her hand on her hip, looking from father to son. Will sniggered briefly while Jacob straightened up and stared at her enigmatically.

'Tell me, Jacob.'

'Is it no longer considered ill-natured to question the host about the victuals he offers to his guests?'

'Not if the guest suspects the victuals to have been stolen,' Eleanor said steadily.

'Stolen, mistress?'

Although he spoke quietly, Eleanor became aware that the whole family had stopped what they were doing in order to listen. All eyes were on her.

'That's what I said.'

'Stolen is a harsh word,' Jacob murmured. 'And one that I prefer not to hear spoken beneath my roof.'

She drew a deep breath, prepared to challenge the word *my*, then decided to let it be. Turning aside she saw Mary continue to stir the saucepan while Dorcas heaped the bread in a pile in the middle of the table.

'So come now – set to!' ordered Jacob, rubbing his hands. 'Girl, set out the platters and the forks. Mary, leave the pot and light the candles'– he indicated Eleanor's silver candelabra – 'and you boy – hand me down the platter and hold it steady now . . .'

Everyone hurried to obey him. Mary lit the candles with a spill from the fire and Dorcas returned from the kitchen with a pile of plates. She set them out with a fork placed crosswise on each, then added one of Eleanor's afternoon teacups to each place. The boy Ned reached down the beautiful pewter dish that hung over the fireplace, put it on the carpet in front of the hearth and Eleanor stoically averted her eyes from the mess that was made before Jacob and Will had succeeded in transferring the smoking, sizzling pig on to it. The carpet in front of the fireplace was now slippery with grease.

'Seating – come now, where's the seating?'

Ned and the other children collected the dining chairs, dragging at them gleefully and then arguing about which one went where, while the boy Will threw another armful of telegraph pole logs on the fire. The heat was intense, and everyone was sweating freely.

Not only that, everyone was busy; everyone was laughing and talking, red-faced and smarting-eyed as they hurried to and fro, and the only person with nothing to do was Eleanor. Superfluous as an old shoe, she stood by the dead telephone and watched helplessly as her own era dissolved and the brutish world of the sixteenth-century yeoman gradually took its place. Unbelieving, and yet somehow resigned, she could only try hard to smile and tell herself that it served her right.

Staggering from the fire with the pig on its big dish Jacob narrowly missed dropping it when one of the little girls cannoned in to him. He set it down on the table with a crash that made the candles leap.

'The time is ripe when we all fall to!' he bawled. 'All to the table and each to his place! Mistress, be seated on my right hand as befits a guest of honour . . .'

She moved forward slowly, aware that it would be unwise to appear in any way ungracious, and standing at the head of the table Jacob began to carve quickly and roughly as the children scrambled to seat themselves. They watched their father with greedy anticipation, pinching and nudging one another (Little carnivores, thought Eleanor), and at the foot of the table Mary stood by the big saucepan ladling out what looked like dumplings and gravy. She still wore the tea towel wrapped round her head. When everyone had been served Jacob threw down the carving knife with a clatter, then clasped his greasy hands together and closed his eyes. Everyone, including Eleanor, followed suit.

'Praise the Lord, ye servants; O praise the name of the Lord. Blessed be the name of the Lord fromthistimeforth frrrrevermoreAmen.

The meal began. Chewing enthusiastically Jacob poured a dark liquid from the big kitchen jug into each of the cups as they were passed to him. He raised his own.

'Here's a health and prosperity to this house on St James's Day!'

Resolving to make the best of things, Eleanor drank. And then choked convulsively.

'What in the name of heaven are we drinking?'

Jacob grinned at her, and pointed with a lump of meat to the bottles on the drinks table.

'You've not mixed –' Eleanor sniffed incredulously at her cup, 'you don't mean you've mixed sherry and brandy together?'

She gazed round at them all helplessly. Will and Ned were downing the appalling mixture in hearty imitation of their father, while Mary, she noticed with relief, contented herself with an occasional neat sip. Opposite her, Dorcas was solicitously holding a cup for one of the two smaller girls, and on her left was Jacob, tearing a hunk of bread apart and dabbling it in his gravy. Cheerful and ebullient, she noticed for the first time how his presence seemed to dominate the room and she sat thinking: I've lost. We could never have maintained equality for long, the balance was too difficult and too complicated, but now he's in the ascendancy. He started off with every disadvantage; frightened as a wild animal in a trap only forty-eight hours ago, and look at him now. He can only have done it through sheer power of personality – plus, I suppose, the unspoken back-up power of his family – but I shouldn't have let it happen. I had everything, and somehow I've lost it all. But maybe there's still time – although what do I mean by time, after what's happened? Either there's no such thing or else it's become so disorientated that I can't understand it any more . . .

She was roused by the tapping of Jacob's forefinger on the rim of her plate. 'Eat, mistress. The rest of us began long since.'

She was unable to put it off any longer. Looking down at the large hunk of pork and at the hard, greyish dumplings sitting forlornly in the thin gravy she controlled a shudder and picked up her fork. For a moment she toyed with the idea of going to fetch a knife (one of her *own* knives from

125

her *own* dining-room), then seeing all eyes upon her decided against it. Instead she put down her fork and picked up a lump of meat in her fingers and cautiously bit a piece off. The taste was much better than she had feared; it was tender and juicy and agreeably smoky, and thus emboldened she tried a morsel of dumpling. They were certainly rather heavy, yet they had an elusive spicy taste that was far from unpleasant. She reached for a chunk of bread and copied their method of sopping up the gravy with it.

'So, mistress,' Jacob said, eyeing her over the bone he was chewing. 'Are you well content with what you see of your forebears? Do we please you?'

The conflicting thoughts in her mind made it impossible to reply. She stared at him in silence.

'Do you find us comely, mistress? Kindly, hospitable, sanguine? Or are you perchance disappointed? Discomforted, even? You look at me as if you are in two minds whether to show me the door.' Without haste he detached a bit of meat from a back tooth. 'Rustic, am I then? Boorish? *Brutish?*'

One of the boys sniggered.

'You still haven't told me where you got the pig from,' Eleanor said finally.

Propping his elbows on the table Jacob considered the bone he was now holding in both hands.

'This pig, mistress?'

'Yes.'

'Ah. Well now, there are two likely answers to that question. One is that I brought it with me from whence I came, and the other that I found it committing a trespass on my property?'

'Your property?' She was determined to challenge him this time.

'All depends upon which age we are dwelling in, doesn't it, mistress?'

'We are living in my age, Jacob,' she said. 'You and your family are my guests.'

He took an unhurried draught from his tea cup and then sat back, smacking his lips. 'Of course, mistress. Be it

126

whatever you say, to be sure. And now let me cut for you another portion from the sucking pig that the woman and I bought in the big market place that is holy as a church and big as a parliament house . . .'

He pulled the dish towards him and began to carve off some more rough slices. Immediately all his family held out their plates. Ignoring them, he extended a dripping gob of port impaled on the fork to Eleanor.

'No thank you, Jacob.'

'You must eat, mistress.'

She sat back, pushing her plate away. 'You gave me too much to begin with.'

'I said – eat, mistress.'

'And I said – no thank you.'

The tension mounted as they stared at one another, then very slowly and without taking his eyes from her face Jacob moved the fork in the direction of the two boys. One of them seized the meat in his fingers and the other tried to grab it from him. They lost it under the table. Laughing drunkenly they scuffled about on the floor. Still staring at Eleanor, Jacob prodded beneath the table with the fork and one of the boys bellowed with pain. Continuing to hold out their plates, the rest of the family shrieked with laughter.

Suddenly hysterical, Eleanor banged her fist on the table. 'Stop it – stop it!'

They quietened, and sat staring at her in wonderment. Jacob continued to carve the pig and to pass chunks of it down the length of the table.

'Please . . .' Eleanor said, forcing back the tears. 'Please stop trying to turn me into a different sort of person all the time. I keep seeing myself as some kind of prim maiden aunt confronted by soccer hooligans – I'm sorry, what I mean is, you make it so hard for me to behave naturally, somehow. Perhaps it's just a sign that I'm feeling a bit outnumbered . . .'

She looked round at them appealingly, but Mary avoided her eyes and the two little girls were busy trying to stuff pellets of bread down the necks of one another's tee-shirts. Her gaze lingered on Dorcas, willing her back to the fleeting intimacy of the alphabet lesson, but there was no response. Pink-faced and laughing, she had eyes only for her father.

The boys hauled themselves up from under the table, and pulling her plate towards her again Eleanor attempted to eat a little more. But the pork and dumplings were now congealing in a greasy mess and she had no appetite.

'I suppose it was stupid of me to believe that there's no real difference between us, that the difference in time doesn't matter,' she continued, addressing herself to Jacob. 'Of course it matters. In fact, it should be a source of wonderment and joy. Yet even in our world now you'll find that a lot of cruel and unnecessary suffering is being caused by people of different races and creeds who live together but refuse to show tolerance towards each other's outlook. They dislike each other for such silly reasons – difference in cooking, ways of dressing, not to mention colour of skin and the accents in which they speak.'

She waited, hoping that one of them might show some curiosity about the idea of people with different coloured skins, but no one did. Then she told herself to stop *teaching*, for after all this was a festive occasion, when laughter was more important than earnest discussion. Yet having started, it seemed as if she couldn't stop.

'Differences are *good,* and I can't bear the marvellous and exciting differences between you and me to become debased into a cheap and nasty kind of class thing, like how you hold your knife and fork or which daily paper you read. I know I've got cross with you all once or twice, and I'm sorry, but you must see that there's such a tremendous amount you've got to learn purely for your own good, and if you're going to live permanently in this century – my century – you'll have to meet the modern world at least half way. And I believe that you could do it – pay lip service to it, if you like – without surrendering any of your own culture or your own personalities. It could be fun, and a very interesting project for you, and all I can say again and again is that if you're willing to learn I'll do everything within my power to help you.'

No one made any comment, and the ensuing silence was

finally broken by Jacob, who belched loudly.

'Have the next one on me,' muttered Eleanor.

'A farmer over Grafton way fathered five children on his dairymaid and her not above three-and-twenty,' Jacob remarked.

'That wasn't quite what I meant,' Eleanor said wearily. Now that the eating had slowed in most cases to a halt, she wished that they could leave the table. But Jacob refilled his teacup from the kitchen jug before pushing it hospitably towards her.

'And where are your children, mistress?' he asked suddenly. 'With your husband dead, why are they not here to offer aid and comfort?'

'I have no children,' she told him quietly.

They all looked at her, even the little girls, and it was painfully obvious that the idea of a woman without children was a curious one.

'No children, mistress?' pursued Jacob. 'How then? Surely the coupling of man and woman, duck and drake, dog and bitch has the same outcome?'

'Unfortunately not in my case.' She was determined to treat the matter lightly. 'I am probably what you would call barren.'

One of the boys sniggered. Without looking at him Jacob fetched him a clout on the ear.

'Say on, mistress.'

'What more is there to say? Except that I don't propose discussing my personal life with you and your family.'

'Personal?' He frowned. 'What is personal?'

'I believe it comes from the Latin. In this particular case it means private. Something that is no concern of anyone else.'

He sat with his teacup held in both hands, taking a leisurely sip every now and then while he eyed her over the rim. 'Poor, poor lady,' he said.

'I don't need your pity, Jacob,' she said steadily. 'I live in a world where women do more than bear a child a year to justify their existence.'

'Our ways are better.'

'So it's come to that, after all,' she replied sadly. 'The

129

question of which is best. And that's only a stone's throw away from I'm right, you're wrong.'

'We can't live in two ages at once, mistress.'

'But need it be a source of contention between us? By that I mean, must we quarrel . . .'

He turned from her, staring heavily down the length of the table. Wax from the candles had dripped into pools on the polished wood, but among all the other greasy mess it scarcely noticed. The fire had subsided to a red glow in a desert of hot white ash and one of the little girls had fallen asleep across the table with her head almost in her plate.

'It's high time someone put that child to bed,' Eleanor observed.

No one moved. Finally Jacob roused himself. 'To bed? No one goes to bed on the Feast of St James! After the eating there is dancing—'

He drained his cup and then stood up rather unsteadily. Walking round to the sleeping child he picked her up and she dangled from under his arm like a kitten. The other children gathered round him while Mary began to collect the plates together and Eleanor remained seated.

'Do you have a fiddle, mistress? Or a flute?'

'I'm sorry,' she said.

Dropping his little daughter unceremoniously on the floor he went over to the fire and kicked the logs together. A shower of sparks flew up and flames reappeared. Despite the warmth of the evening he threw some more wood on.

'That's sad news. Perhaps you can sing for us, mistress? Can you sing Catkins are Green-O, or My Lady Betty's Fancy?'

'I'm afraid not. The best I can do is to offer a little canned music—'

Leaving the table she went over to the bookshelf and took down the portable radio. She switched it on, scanning the stations while Jacob and the children gathered round, intrigued but not frightened.

'I'm afraid that's the best I can do,' she said as a thin squeal of pop music filled the room.

It seemed to galvanise them into action. Staggering, the two boys pushed back the table and thrust the chairs aside.

130

The little girl who had lain whimpering on the floor stood up, rubbing her eyes, while Dorcas smoothed her hair and tucked her tee-shirt back in her skirt.

'Come, Mary – leave the pots to their own devices,' Jacob shouted impatiently. 'Form up – set to your partners . . . you, boy, to your sister there . . .'

Whistling, he pushed the children into a country dance formation then shouted again for Mary, and when she appeared he seized her by the waist and capered her round. The hop-and-skip dance fitted the pop beat perfectly and the children laughed and clapped as their parents spun between the furniture, breathless and giddy.

The noise increased, and when Jacob danced Mary into the waiting arms of Ned he turned, breathless and sweating, to Eleanor.

'On your toes, mistress – let's have you tripping a measure! Dancing belongs to all ages and conditions of man and woman.'

He grabbed at her, and holding her in a grip of iron leaped with her in and out of the firelight while the children giggled and jigged nearby. Dizzily aware of Dorcas partnered by the panting Will, and of Mary – with the tea towel still shrouding her hair – bobbing on the arm of Ned, she began to laugh wildly, suddenly exultantly happy to be sharing the family's pleasure.

The miracle of their presence came back to her, and when the music was interrupted by a newsflash about a lorry shedding its load on the A604 and Jacob picked up the radio and bawled into it: 'The music, the music, you lumpkin!' she laughed until the tears filled her eyes.

When the music returned he dropped the radio back on the table with a satisfied grunt, convinced that he was being obeyed, and then grabbed at Eleanor again. This time he put both arms round her waist and hugged her closely to him and the heat of his body burning through the flowered shirt made her suddenly mad for him. The feeling hadn't happened to her since before Mo died, and the strength of it, together with the modest amount of sherry-brandy she had drunk, drove away all reason. With her arms round his neck she hopped weakly from one foot to the other while

131

she sought to lose herself in his hard, sweating, living beauty. His hair flicked her cheek and she pressed her nose into his bare neck, hungrily absorbing everything of him that she could. She closed her eyes, and when she opened them again the whole room seemed bathed in the livid, leaping glare from the fire. The drinks table overturned with a crash that sounded very far away and then she became aware of Will lying outstretched and helpless on the floor, his eyes unfocused and his lips working foolishly. Feet were dancing over him and on top of him, and beneath the laughter and desire and the hectic spinning gaiety she somehow glimpsed the first hint of savagery.

It sobered her abruptly, and with a stammered excuse that she felt breathless she tore herself from Jacob's grasp and stumbled out of the room.

3

The garden seemed very dark and very quiet and she lifted her face gratefully to a breath of wind that stirred the glimmering roses.

Gradually her heart stopped its pounding, and with the desire faded she leaned back against the gate and looked at the cottage. Firelight and candlelight combined to illuminate the laughing capering figures inside with an extraordinary brilliance and she reminded herself that social historians would give all they possessed to be in her place.

She watched the silhouette of Dorcas dart out of the lighted front door, closely followed by that of Jacob. He was stumbling now, and the girl dodged him round one of the mounds of clipped box before running back indoors again. Following her, Jacob collided violently with either Will or Ned who was in the act of rushing out with his hand over his mouth. When she heard him being explosively sick in one of the flower beds Eleanor squeamishly turned her head away.

A heavy crash from inside the sitting-room made her

start. Instinctively she ran towards it, and on the threshold
she stopped dead. One of the big glass lamps lay shattered
on the floor and by the light of the leaping fire flames she
saw that Jacob had caught and imprisoned Dorcas. The
front of her Marks & Spencers dress had been torn open to
reveal her immature young breasts and Jacob's other hand
was fumbling urgently beneath her skirt. She was standing
with her legs apart, and if there was horror in Jacob's
panting sweating lasciviousness there was far more in the
girl's air of resigned acquiescence.

'Jacob Dawes, you drunken sot—' Eleanor's voice
cracked.

Quickly the girl broke free and slipped across the room
to where other members of the family were grouped in
silence, and with a fresh sense of outrage Eleanor realised
that Mary was among them, and had been watching the
incident with the same mute acquiescence.

She walked slowly into the ravaged room and halted in
front of Jacob. Already the heat of her rage was cooling and
solidifying, and she stood contemplating him with a sort of
calm repugnance.

'It's time for you to go,' she said very quietly and calmly.
'I don't know how you came here, but you'll have to go by
the same route. Go now. If you want blankets or money or
food I will give you what I can, but it's imperative that you
leave my house now. You have brought a kind of ver-
minous chawbacon anarchy into my life which I can no
longer tolerate. So pick up your child,' she pointed to the
little girl who lay curled asleep on the grease-stained
hearth, 'take all the things that I gave you, only go *now*.'

He seemed to sober up even as she was speaking. Pulling
his shoulders back he stopped swaying, then wiped the cuff
of his shirt across his face.

'Where then do you advise we should go?'

She shrugged. 'That's your affair. I can only suggest that
you go back to where you came from.'

'But therein lies the riddle. It took no effort of my will to
bring us here, and now—' He rubbed his sleeve over his
face again and she saw that his eyes were haggard.

'I don't care where you go,' she reiterated coldly. 'Just

133

go, and leave me in peace.'

'There is no peace in your breast, mistress,' he said slowly. 'There is no heart in it, either. Nothing but a little hard stone from the supermarket.'

'Will you please *go!*' She stamped her foot. 'We'll say nothing about the wilful damage, the trail of wreckage that you leave behind – that was the price I had to pay for inviting you in.'

'And now you are casting us out?' There was a piteousness about him which she refused to acknowledge. She folded her arms and stared at him unflinchingly.

'If you like to put it that way.'

On the other side of the room she heard Mary burst into tears. The children clustered round her, patting and stroking her, and there was a clumsy tenderness in the way in which the boy Ned tried to staunch her tears with the tips of his fingers. Brushing past Eleanor Jacob went over to them, then with his arm round Mary turned to look at her again.

'Mistress – in the name of our Lord God—'

'Don't forget the baby,' Eleanor said. 'I can hear it crying.'

She had never felt stronger or more in control of a situation, and she waited impassively as Mary went slowly across to the staircase followed by the children. They began to ascend towards the sound of the baby's voice, and Jacob, at the tail end of the little procession, halted at the foot of the stairs with his hand cupping the rough ball-shape on the end of the baluster rail.

'I carved this,' he said. 'I shaped it from the heart of an elm that stood close by its brother in my field.'

'Twenty-four hours ago I wanted to hear you say things like that,' she replied slowly. 'I wanted you to tell me about building the house, about what you thought and felt and how you lived . . .'

'But was it not better to show you? The woman and I were much pleased to prepare tonight's carouse in your honour, but now I see the truth of it. We wanted to show you, to make you part of our company and our ways, but you only wanted to hear tell of it.'

She stirred a sprinkling of broken glass with her foot. 'Can you blame me?'

'May we stay until first light, mistress?'

She stood watching the hand tracing the end of the baluster rail. The hand that had carved it. The man who had built the house with his own strength and love . . . She reminded herself of these things, but the magic had gone. The whole extraordinary experience now seemed merely wearisome and distasteful and the sooner the thing was ended the better.

'I'm sorry, Jacob,' she said, quite gently.

Without another word he turned and went upstairs.

Relieved of their presence she stood contemplating the room. The fire had died down to a few blue flames licking at the ash-powdered logs. Ash seemed to cover everything. Although the windows and the front door were still open the air was heavy with the smell of food, and moths and other small winged creatures of the night were dancing round the low-flickering candles. Dripped wax was building up on the table, but she made no attempt to blow them out; the damage had been done, and a little more was neither here nor there, but when she became aware that the radio was still playing she switched it off and replaced it on the bookshelf.

Standing at the foot of the staircase she listened for the sound of voices, but the place was silent. Even the baby had stopped its crying.

Perhaps, she thought with a leap of the heart, they had already gone. Dematerialized in some abrupt sort of way that would save the need for formal goodbyes. Then her straining ears caught the soft creak of a floorboard overhead. They were still there.

Dusting ash and food crumbs from an armchair she sat down to wait. The newspaper lay close by and she picked it up and began to scan the headlines for the second time that day. In spite of her calm the silence began to bite into her nerves and she felt a small muscle jumping in her cheek. She opened the paper and forced herself to read an article about Common Market economics, but it seemed as if all her attention was concentrated in her ears.

The click of a bedroom latch came like a faraway pistol shot, and she carried on reading while the slow drag of footsteps passed along the corridor that led to the head of the staircase. Forcing her eyes to travel down the column of print she listened to the unhurried descent, the footsteps so close that they could have been taken for the slow shuffling of some large multi-legged animal. When the sound ceased she slowly lowered the newspaper and looked over the top of it.

They were standing in a close group at the foot of the stairs, looking at her, and with a sudden prickle of apprehension she realised that they had all changed back into their old drab homespun. Mary, with the baby in her arms, was shrouded in her cloak, and once again her nostrils caught the strange elusive scent of herbs and old damp stonework.

Mesmerised, she could only stare back at them, and it was not until Jacob slowly raised his arm and flung something at her that she found herself capable of movement. Jerking to her feet she ducked aside, then saw that he had thrown their new clothes, rolled up in a bundle. It landed close to her feet and came undone, a spilling heap of flowered cotton, tartan, Mickey-mouse tee-shirts and dark blue denim. A toothbrush bounded into the pile of broken glass from the lamp.

'I told you that you could keep . . .' Eleanor began.

'We want no more part in your work,' Jacob said. 'What you told us is lies.'

'Lies?' She remained standing, the newspaper still in her hands.

'All this,' Jacob said, indicating the once beautiful room. 'We know the real truth of it – the lights that come and go, the water that obeys you up the stairs and down, the voice in the little casket – we can explain the true workings of it.'

'I'd be interested to hear.' Somehow she forced herself to remain calm.

'So be it.' He paused for a moment. 'It's witchcraft.'

'*Witchcraft?*' The newspaper slipped from her fingers. 'Jacob, for God's sake. You don't believe in witchcraft any more than I do.'

136

He came slowly towards her, followed in a tightly protective group by his family. She felt the colour leave her face.

'Jacob – Mary . . . children!'

She turned and began to run towards the door; hesitated, and then dashed to the phone. The receiver was in her hand before she remembered that it was disconnected.

'*Get the witch!*'

They were between her and the front door now, and there wasn't time to reach the kitchen. She flung herself at the open window and her collection of Staffordshire figures crashed to the floor. She had one knee through when they reached her and dragged her back. She was a strong woman and she fought hard for her life, but there seemed to be something almost demonic about the hands that caught her and held her. Through the pain and the terror she could sense the smallness of some of them – the pretty child fingers bruising her flesh, the little nails tearing and clawing as she was hauled towards the front door.

With a last effort she swung round in their grasp and looked into their faces, but there was no pity. Beneath the sounds of excited panting she heard a low snigger from one of the boys as her dress rode up over her thighs. She heard herself say 'Please . . . *please* . . .' then felt the palm of a hand seal her mouth. She bit it, and hacked furiously with her feet at the legs that surrounded her.

Then they lifted her, Jacob and the two boys, and held her aloft. The massive lintel of the front door caught her upturned face and she screamed with pain. They laughed and dashed with her through the garden, trampling the lavender and heedless of the tearing rose thorns.

She was almost unconscious when the last moment came, and her final cry seared the night and fled away over the valley, startling the owls and disturbing a fox in the destruction of a young rabbit.

4

'You'll like her,' Eric Seward was saying to Corinne.

The springs of the old blue Mini squeaked and the windows rattled as they bounced over the potholes. 'She's very friendly and sympathetic and she's certainly got a feeling for history.'

'Does she know you're bringing me?'

'No. She doesn't know either of us is coming, but I do want you to meet.'

'Hope I'll come up to scratch,' she said laconically and he gave her knee an affectionate squeeze.

'She'll think you're great.'

Corinne had been back for five days and once again life had swung from the mean and dishevelled to the idyllic. They had spent as much time in bed as children and office would allow, and in between love-making she had set about cleaning the house, washing their clothes and cooking good meals. He took a day off, ostensibly because of family business, but just so that he could treat himself to the pleasure of being close to her, and share the marvel of how everything seemed to come alive at her touch. Whistling, she made puff pastry and a sponge cake with striped ice cream in the middle for the children. She sewed some new bathroom curtains, and she used the tee-shirt with *I Like It!* printed on it to polish the windows. The black eye faded to an agreeable look of heavy-lidded sensuousness, the cut healed on her cheek, and her hair, which he lovingly shampooed for her under the shower, was like a cloud of soft curly silk.

To take her to meet Eleanor Millard seemed an excellent idea.

They reached the end of the lane where the land fell away to the small valley crammed with ripening corn.

138

'Look,' he said, indicating the cottage behind the hedge. 'Isn't it a beauty?'

She peered through the windscreen, then said: 'Is that her car over there?'

'My God—' He got out of the Mini and went over to it. Still on its side in the ditch it lay framed in ferns and pink campion and the shower of crisp dead leaves that had been torn from their branches. Crouching, he looked in through the smashed side window and was disturbed to see that the keys were still in the ignition. With Corinne by his side he went through the open front gate and up the path, calling her name.

She was obviously at home because the windows were wide open. So was the door. He knocked, and then looked round it.

'Jesus Christ,' Corinne said.

White-faced he walked into the sitting-room, trying speechlessly to assimilate the shock. The gracious golden room was a nightmare jumble of smashed furniture, broken glass and torn curtains. White ash from the fire-place speckled everything, and on the dining table, which had evidently been dragged in from the other room, was the remains of a roast pig on a big pewter dish. The head, with its blind eye sockets and wide grimacing mouth, had an extraordinarily bestial appearance and he recoiled sharply from the dense cloud of flies that suddenly rose from it. The place stank.

'Well, well,' Corinne said slowly. 'It must have been quite some party!'

With the toe of her shoe she prodded at the spilled bundle of clothes that lay on the floor. Jeans, tee-shirts, a flowered dress. 'A naughty nudie party, at that.'

'But it couldn't have – I mean, she wasn't that sort—'

'Wasn't?'

'Something's happened to her. Something terrible . . .'

Regaining his power of movement he dashed through the cottage, and the devastation was everywhere. Each room spoke of violence, of some inexplicable outrage that had occurred, and he returned breathless and shaking to the open front door.

'If you're sure she's still here we'd better search the garden,' Corinne said, picking her way across the terrible sitting-room. 'I notice the phone's dead.'

The heat was stifling in the garden, but at least the smell was better. They hurried along the little winding paths through the shrub roses to the old fruit trees and Corinne, more intrigued than frightened, put her arm round his waist.

'It's all so awful – so *awful* . . .' he kept saying.

'She was probably on holiday and squatters moved in.'

'But she didn't say anything about going away.'

They found nothing except two or three small toys – a plastic doll and a handful of coloured building bricks – and they came to a halt at the boundary hedge that gave on to the sea of motionless blue-green corn.

'What's in that long grass over there?' Shielding her eyes, she pointed.

He moved towards it, remembering as he did so that Eleanor had shown him the pond, and said what a pity it was that it had dried up.

I'd like to have ducks and goldfish, she had said.

He noticed that the grass had been trampled in places, and then he saw a woman's sandal lying close by. Sick with premonition he peered through the thin towering leaves of reed mace, and there she was. She was lying on her back on the dry cracked clay of the pond with her arms outflung as if in supplication. Her flesh had a bleached, slightly luminous appearance and her open eyes were blank and colourless as blobs of aspic. Breaking through the reeds he scrambled closer, but although he stretched out his hands he hadn't the courage to touch her. Choking, he became aware that Corinne had seized his arm and was pulling him away.

'It's no use, you can't do anything,' she was saying over and over again, as if to a child. 'It's far too late to do anything now . . .'

They drove back to the town without speaking, and he was parking the Mini in the police station forecourt when Corinne finally broke the silence.

'I take it you were screwing her.'

'For God's sake – what makes you say a thing like that?'

'You bloody fool,' she said, 'you're crying.'

Bunty Parsloe was on all fours in the vicarage kitchen garden picking peas. Dwarf peas were convenient because they didn't need staking, but the snag was that with every year that passed, stooping, squatting or kneeling became a little more onerous. *Take what you want, said God: take it and pay for it.* It seemed a reasonable enough principle to her, and next year she thought she might go back to standard height peas again.

And then remembered that she wouldn't be here, this time next year.

Neither she nor Arthur had referred to the scene in the church which had taken place ten days ago; possibly each was waiting for the other, yet instinct told her that for her to re-open the subject would more than likely be construed as fussing interference and would get them nowhere. There were signs, however, to indicate that he still intended to leave the ministry. On Wednesday morning he cancelled the parochial church council meeting for that evening, and passing the open study door on Friday she heard him telephone the diocesan bishop's secretary and request an interview with his lordship as soon as possible. It was a personal matter of some urgency, he said. And then on Sunday, when he would have been taking morning service supposing there had been a congregation, he had spent the time sorting through piles of old ecclesiastical books and making a bonfire of them on what used to be the tennis court. Although silent and withdrawn he seemed quite calm, and there was no animosity in his tone when he spoke to her now and then. Although his breath smelt she didn't think he 'had been drunk any more since that terrible day, but he looked far from well and she was deeply concerned about the look of suffering in his eyes.

She prayed for him at many odd moments during the course of the day, speaking simply and without undue preamble to the heavenly Father whom she had always thought of as a wise and loving friend, but when bedtime came she no longer said her prayers at the bedside; in view of Arthur's spiritual unrest she said them in the bathroom, kneeling on the parquet lino facing the towel rail after she had cleaned her teeth. She generally ended with the Creed, but on the last two nights had added the third Collect, for Aid against all Perils.

The colander was full of peas and she began to walk back to the vicarage. The earth was pale and parched by the sun, and this morning they had said on the wireless that no hoses were to be used for watering gardens or for washing cars. Crossing the weedy drive she was surprised to see a blue Mini turn in through the gates and come hesitantly towards her. She stood waiting as a tall young man uncoiled himself from the driving seat.

'I'm very sorry to trouble you, but I wonder if I could see the vicar?'

There was a strange air about him that made her feel curiously uneasy; it also had the effect of alerting her protective instinct.

'I am Mrs Parlsoe,' she said, 'and I'm not quite sure where my husband is at the moment. Perhaps I could help in the meantime?'

The young man opened his mouth and then closed it again. She observed, not without sympathy, that some sort of struggle was taking place in his mind.

'I want to consult him about a burial,' he said finally.

'A parishioner?' she asked, startled.

He nodded bleakly. 'A Mrs Millard, who bought Jackdaw's Cottage – I believe she came to see him about—'

She recoiled with a cry of shocked distress, and a number of peas spilled over the edge of the colander and bounded on to the drive. 'Not the young Mrs Millard who – oh dear. Oh dear, how very dreadful. An accident?'

'We don't know. No one seems to know what to think. The police—'

'Police?'

'Yes – they won't say much at the moment and they're keeping it away from the press because you see it's all so terrible and – and extraordinary. I mean, who were all the people who had obviously been there – where did they go to? And most of all, how did she come to *drown?* The post mortem showed superficial cuts and bruises but made it quite clear that death was caused by drowning. *Drowning . . . but the pond was bone dry!*'

She stood staring at him with her hands clasped tightly round the colander. In the twinkling sunlight that shone down through the trees his face looked taut with worry.

'Was Mrs Millard a relative?' she asked finally.

'No. Just a friend. I don't believe she had any close family, but someone's got to accept responsibility for – for the arrangements and somehow it seems to me very important for her to have an old-fashioned Christian burial in the village where she had made her home, and that it should be conducted by a priest who could also throw some sort of – well, spiritual light on what happened. You see, I can't help feeling that there's some sort of religious explanation – why I think this I don't know, because I'm afraid that I'm not really a believer myself, but—'

'Listen,' she said gently, 'suppose you tell me all about it from the very beginning. I don't even know your name . . .'

He finished the story, so far as he knew it, in the dusty, cluttered sitting-room. With his back to the door he was unaware that anyone else had entered the room until he saw the loving smile that suddenly illuminated his companion's rather homely features.

'Arthur, my dear,' she said. 'This young man has come to find you because he needs your help and strength. Perhaps you will comfort him while I go and make some tea.'

He was rather surprised that they should press him to stay to supper, and he saw them wave from the porch as he drove away. The funeral was fixed for Monday at 2.30 and he tried hard to think of people he could ask to attend. Her bank manager perhaps, and maybe the people from the farm nearby; it was somehow very important that she should be in the presence of friends on that final occasion, but of course, there wasn't time to begin tracing anyone from her teaching days.

Perhaps Corinne would turn up, although he doubted it. Her sudden needling suspicion that he had been having an affair with Eleanor had exploded into a row which had gone on intermittently throughout the night, and on the following morning she had announced her intention of going up to London for the day. He hadn't seen her since, but there was always the odd chance that she might be back by the time he reached home.

But whether she was or she wasn't seemed to matter very little, and he drove along the quiet road in a mood of resignation that bordered on tranquillity. A splendid moon was shedding its glistening light over the countryside and he couldn't help thinking what a very decent and dependable sort of chap that vicar was.